HAMILTON PLACE

Liz,
My Very Best
Always to my
"Special" friend

Love
Mary Theohold Reinhart

HAMILTON PLACE

Mary Theodore Reinhart

Writer's Showcase
New York Lincoln Shanghai

Hamilton Place

Writer's Showcase
an imprint of iUniverse, Inc.

For information address:
iUniverse, Inc.
2021 Pine Lake Road, Suite 100
Lincoln, NE 68512
www.iuniverse.com

ISBN: 0-595-26210-4

Printed in the United States of America

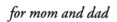

for mom and dad

CHAPTER I

─────────────── ▼ ───────────────

He was tired of fighting the Turks! The year was 1916. The handsome young sailor stood quietly on the deck of the Greek Naval vessel, the St. Georges, his friend and shipmate Nicholas beside him. It had been over a month since the St. Georges had sailed from the city of Pereous in Greece.

Anthony John Pafitis stood in awe of the New York harbor. He could only imagine what lay beyond the wooden dock and warehouses hidden from view. There had been many discussions among his shipmates during the voyage about this city in the New World. And so, he stood there silently, gaining courage with every moment. His olive skin, jet black hair and moustache were a beautiful contrast to the stark white of his navy cap. Anthony was no coward, he simply wanted a better life. Were his thoughts so vivid that his friend Nicholas beside him could hear them? Did he trust his friend enough to share these thoughts? Could it be possible that they shared the same thoughts?

Anthony had seen his share of battle. As his hand moved slowly down his side his fingers touched the bullet that had never been removed from his leg. The force of the second bullet piercing the right side of his neck from which he carried a very visible scar was still fresh in his memory. He had seen too many of his friends die! He knew that the Turks were his enemies, he was never entirely sure why the two countries were at war, but he was sure that they were definitely people to be hated.

This place called New York would be an escape from the fighting and surely must hold a better life for a young man of 23. He loved his country; the island of Cypros, (Cyprus) where he was born on September 5, 1892, and the beautiful city of Athens where he had spent many wonderfully happy days. His mind turned to thoughts of his older brother George and how much he had depended upon him since the loss of his parents. But now he was a man, a sailor who had done battle and despite the love he felt for his brother and for his country, his decision had been made. The ship was leaving New York harbor tomorrow evening and he had no time for these doubts that kept haunting his mind.

He turned toward Nicholas, the friend of his youth, looking deep into his eyes, hoping somehow to predict his reaction. Was he making a mistake trusting his friend? While still agonizing over his decision, without realizing, he put his future at stake and spoke the words he had held back throughout the voyage to his friend. He did not intend to return to Greece! He would leave "the old country" behind in hopes of finding a better life in this "New Land".

Surprisingly, it was not difficult to convince Nicholas. The two had shared their feelings of futility regarding the war with the Turks many times during the past few months. His determination was strengthened with the knowledge that his friend would be beside him.

The two men contrived a very simple plan. Upon disembarking the next morning for shore leave, they would find a place to purchase civilian clothing and make their way inland as quickly as possible. Anthony John Pafitous would search for his friend, John Psirianos who had come to New York almost a year before. John Psirianos had promised to help Anthony find work when and if he could find a way to come to America. He would teach him the ways of this new country. He assured Nicholas that he would also find work, for America was a country where jobs were plentiful.

Before going below to their bunks the two men made a solemn vow to, someday with the help of God, return to their beloved Greece.

So began the longest night of their young lives with neither of the men finding restful sleep. Their thoughts were of Athens, Cypros and the family and friends they were leaving behind. Throughout the night, despite their efforts to quiet them, the questions and doubts could not be stilled. Would their friends and families understand? Would their actions bring them shame? What would happen if they failed?

The morning passed rather quickly as the two men mechanically went about the morning regimen, the planned escape their only thought. Fearing that a large duffel bag would arouse questions, they took only one small bag with a few cherished possessions and a sandwich they had smuggled from the kitchen. Finally the time arrived and they were on the deck with their shipmates awaiting the sound of the bell announcing shore leave.

Anthony John reluctantly looked at the faces of the men with whom he had become as brothers. Faces of men he had come to depend upon for his very life in battle. He wondered if he would ever see his shipmates again. He starred at each face, memorizing each feature as the men chatted away about the days planned activities. One of his friends Harry asked, "Hey, Tony, how will you celebrate your 24th birthday?" Another of the men teased, "Oh, I bet I know what he plans to do"! At this, Harry snatched Anthony's cap from his head and it was being tossed back and forth among his shipmates. The laughter and teasing were most welcome and momentarily broke his tension, although it further added to his feeling of guilt at leaving these men behind. His heart ached to say goodbye to his friends; to ask their forgiveness for what he was about to do.

With the sounding of the bell announcing shore leave, Nicholas and Anthony picked up the small bags and walked down the gangplank in line with their shipmates. With each step, the old life and their homeland became more distant. It was sheer coincidence, yet it seemed appropriate that this new beginning should occur on his 24th birthday. Anthony's foot reached the last step on the gangplank and the moment had arrived; on September 5th, 1916, he stepped for the last time, from the ship that represented his homeland, his past, and he took his first step into his new country, The United States of America.

Trying to remain calm, but constantly watching behind them, the two men followed their plan walking at a casual yet hurriedly pace inland, further and further away from the harbor, stopping only once, to eat the sandwiches they had smuggled from the ship. As the sun began to set they found themselves on a hillside overlooking the New York harbor. In the distant they could see their ship, the St. Georges preparing to leave. As the ship moved slowly from the dock, they experienced the full realization that now, indeed, there was no turning back. They remained standing there watching silently as the outline of the St. Georges become smaller and smaller. With all the courage they could muster, they turned their backs on the last glimpse of their ship and their country and began their life in America.

CHAPTER 2

▼

With much difficulty, since neither could speak the English language very well, they eventually found the address on the slip of paper Anthony had carried from Greece only to learn that his friend, John Psirianos had moved to Canton, Ohio just weeks before. Their money about to be depleted, the two men were forced to find work on their own. With so many immigrants entering the country at that time, it was not uncommon to find those with little or no knowledge of the English language. Employers were used to dealing with all types of dialects, therefore as long as one were not choosy, work was not too difficult to find.

They took one menial job after another always heading in the direction of the state of Ohio. They arrived in Canton, Ohio toward the end of October, 1916 and were able to locate John Psirianos. He had written to Anthony informing him of his move however the ship had left Greece before the letter could reach him. John Psirianos had shocking news for the two men. He had learned that their ship, the St. Georges, during the return voyage to Greece, was lost at sea with no survivors. Anthony was devastated at the thought of Harry and his other shipmates, whose faces would remain with him forever.

Why had he and Nicholas been spared? Was it just mere coincidence that led them from the ship that day, or perhaps the decision had been made for them. Were they meant to survive? Had he confided in Harry, would he have left the ship with him and been spared? These and many more questions would haunt him for the remainder of his life. Certainly his brother George and his family and friends would believe him to be lost at sea as well.

John Psirianos lived up to his promise and found Anthony a job as a cook and Nicholas a job in a warehouse. They worked very hard to learn the ways and language of their new country.

In June 1919, Anthony was becoming restless and did not feel it was safe to remain in one place for very long, therefore he decided he would move to Pittsburgh, Pennsylvania where, rumors were many Greek immigrants had settled. Nicholas had found a woman with whom he was very much in love and so decided he would remain in Canton. The two friends parted but not before promising to keep in touch with one another.

CHAPTER 3

▼

My father lived those years with the fear of being deported at any time. Afraid to use his real name, he assumed the name of Antonios Theodorou, (Anthony Theodore) He spent the next several years living in many rooms and apartments in and around the Pittsburgh area from June, 1919 until April, 1926 at which time, according to his records, he returned to New York City. He would remain there until May, 1928, at which time he again moved back to Pittsburgh where he would remain for the rest of his life.

Among the few items he brought with him from Greece was a cherished picture of his brother George, and a bible written in the Greek language. When he spoke of his homeland, he referred to it only as "the old country".

I would not learn the circumstances of my father's entrance into the United States, his birth name nor that I had an uncle in Greece until my adolescent years.

Although my father had his passport to prove his birth place and his baptismal papers, since he lacked the necessary papers given when one enters the United States through the legal process, despite his many attempts, he could not become a naturalized citizen. He was given papers stating that he was an alien living in the United States that he was instructed to carry with him at all times. When my father lived on the island of Cyprus, it was under British protection. For this reason he would become registered on the 29th day of January 1923 as a British subject at the British Consulate in Pittsburgh, Pennsylvania. Nevertheless, he continued his attempts to become a citizen of the United States.

My father had acquired a job as a cook at a state owned facility referred to as a "Fresh Air Camp" near McKeesport, Pennsylvania. The camp was established by the state to assist persons who had been discharged from a hospital but were still in need of rest, care and recuperation.

Most immigrants would not think of marrying someone outside of their nationality. Even though she was not of Grecian decent, my father was stricken by this thin, beautiful German woman with long dark wavy hair who arrived at the Fresh Air Camp. He felt compassion for Mathilda King and her infant son, both very frail and in need of rest, nourishment and care. The baby, John, had been born on October 5, 1927 in Magee hospital several weeks after Mathilda had been admitted with malnutrition. Anthony quickly decided that he would make it his responsibility to see that they had everything they needed to regain their strength.

Although she was impressed with the sensitivity and caring of this handsome Greek, Mathilda King was very reluctant to become involved with another man. The shame and humiliation she had just experienced with her present husband was still fresh in her mind. Yet, this man with his gentle manner and soft words made her feel wanted and needed as she hadn't for such a long time. And so, she accepted his kindness and friendship and they soon fell in love.

When Mathilda regained her strength and she and her son were able to leave the Fresh Air Camp she obtained a divorce from her husband. Anthony John Theodore and Mathilda Gearing King were soon married. They moved into a small apartment in McKeesport, Pennsylvania.

On November 21, 1929, my sister Annetta Irene was born, followed by Helen Annatessia on February 5, 1931. I was born on January 21, 1933. My father wanted to name me Mary Sophia, my mother was holding out for Marie, after her sister. When the time came for my baptism in the Greek Orthodox Church on Cedar Avenue, the priest took the decision from their hands and named me Maria Sophia Theodore. But, that was not the end of the matter for when my birth certificate arrived, it bore the name, Sophia Maria Theodore. These changes and/or mistakes were not too uncommon at that time. Since my father insisted on calling me Mary, the name Mary Sophia Theodore would eventually be changed on my birth certificate.

CHAPTER 4

▼

During the first two years of my life we lived with some of my father's Grecian friends, the Gianutous family, who lived in the Oakland section of Pittsburgh, Pennsylvania, often referred to as the Soho area. Of course, I have very few recollections of that time. I do remember sitting on a potty behind the door of my parent's bedroom for a very long time, another memory of sitting on my father's lap around a kitchen table, with Mr. Gianutous and his sons. The Gianutous family also could speak very little English, so when the men gathered together it was easier for them to speak their native tongue. They always spoke so loudly that it seemed to a small child that they were always angry. During these conversations, I sat silently with my face hidden in my father's chest. The house was always crowded and very noisy.

In March, 1935, when I was two years old we moved to #9 Hamilton Place, a small secluded section of the North Side of Pittsburgh consisting of two long rows of red brick houses which stood facing one another. A white unevenly laid cobblestone street ran down the center between the two rows of houses. It was so secluded and insignificant that most people were not aware of the existence of Hamilton Place. Walking down Charles Street one might glance into the area, but would stop short of entering.

Each row consisted of eleven connected houses. The houses in the row to the left upon entering were numbered evenly beginning with #2, ending with #22. The opposite side began with #1 ending with #21. We considered the people who lived in the first house of each row to be fortunate for they had their very own porch, while the remaining houses shared a back and front porch, although with their own set of steps on either side. At the far end of Hamilton Place, a low cobblestone wall struggled to hold back the steep wooded hillside. This hillside ran parallel to Charles Street where it eventually ran into to a much longer street named Brighton Road.

A six foot wall with a wide opening in the center announced the entrance of Hamilton Place. The wall partially concealed the houses from passersby.

Charles Street was a major artery when compared to Hamilton Place, just a tiny branch vein or what was referred to as a "paper street" of the North Side. Each house had a small section of backyard with no walls or fences separating them. There was a lower section to the back yards with a pathway leading to an opening in the six foot high cement wall which continued from the front of the rows.

At certain intervals of the back yard were stairs which lead from the upper to the lower section. A large house stood alone separated from the rows, located beyond the lower section of the back yards. For no particular reason except that it was not considered part of Hamilton Place, we saw very little of the family living in the large house.

A neighborhood that seemed isolated from the rest of the world, Hamilton Place was unique in its own way as were its people. The sun seldom reached the cobblestone street between the rows giving the entire area a dark, foreboding appearance. A constant stream of water from the hillside trickled between the white cobblestones adding a cool damp feeling to the already sinister appearance. One dimly lit streetlight clung to a pole at the end of the rows which, when the wind blew, would swing back and forth casting eerie shadows on the houses.

People traveling down Charles Street understandably avoided entering Hamilton Place.

The people of Hamilton Place were mostly immigrants representing many different ethnic backgrounds. To the best of my recollection, in #3 Hamilton Place lived an Italian family named Serra, who had two daughters and two sons; #5 the Manchetti family; #7 the Garvey family; #11 the Thompson family; #13 the Lewis family; and #15 the Bickard family. Across the street were families named Pritchard, Feeney, Neusch, Fisher, Cotton, & Sheets. Since the Garvey family lived next door, Mrs. Garvey and my mother became close friends. Earlene Garvey and I being the same age, generally played together.

A vacant house was quickly filled with a new family since the rent was cheap and housing was scarce. A new family moving in was an exciting event. Looking closely at the windows one could see neighbors peering through slight openings in curtains or from behind white paper blinds. The grownups carefully inspected the newness of the furniture and other belongings, in an attempt to determine the family's financial status, however the children would be interested only in whether or not there would be new kids on the block. Mother would not allow us to go outside during the moving process because the new family would "think we were being nosy", so we stood beside her peeking through the curtains.

It wasn't long after the Barnett family moved into house #19 that they began to build a large wooden fence between their section of back yard and that of #17. The Barnett family had two large dogs and some believed the purpose of the fence was to keep the dogs in, others believed it was to keep the neighbors out. For a while, the fence was the topic of discussion among the adults. Imaginations ran wild with everyone having their own interpretation of the fence. Adding fuel to the suspicions was the fact that the Barnett family was not very friendly. Some neighbors remarked that they seemed to think they were "better than the rest of us". "Why else would they isolate themselves with such a high fence"?

If one of the children approached the fence, a member of the Barnett family would quickly come to the back door and chase them away. The door in the fence was always kept locked. Several times the older boys attempted to climb the fence but were frightened off by Mr. Barnett or his daughter who had a nasty disposition. We used to think she sat in the window all day waiting for someone to venture too close to the fence.

It was difficult to understand some of the people with their "broken English". All were hard working people with the same goal; to eke out a living for their families and never slack their efforts to eventually realize the "American Dream." On warm summer nights when a few neighbors gathered together they often spoke lovingly of their homes in "the old country". Upon entering the United States, most immigrants could neither speak or understand the English language, therefore, they learned from one another, listening to the radio or by any means available. All bills including utilities, rent, labels on cans and boxes, literally everything was written in English, therefore there was no choice but to learn to speak and read the language of their new country.

My father worked as a cook when work was to be had. He had become quite a good cook and later in life, after years of hard work, would earn the title of "master chef". He carried his own set of chef's knives, which were of many different shapes and sizes. These he kept in a small black suitcase out of reach on top of the green kitchen cupboard. We were warned many times never to go near that black suitcase. My father had shown me the knives and the wooden handled knife sharpener many times but I was never allowed to touch them. The knives in the black suitcase would be kept at the restaurant where he would be employed at the time. On days when he came home carrying the small black suitcase, we knew that he had lost his job and we should be very careful not to ask for anything.

Between July 9, 1931 and April 26, 1938 my father served in the National Guard of the United States. In times of disaster, he would be called to report to a camp at nearby Indiantown Gap, Pennsylvania.

During the flood of 1936, my father was called for rescue duty. After several days rescuing stranded people, he came home with a very solemn look upon his face, very much unlike his usual smile upon seeing his family. He seemed very depressed, refused dinner and hardly spoke. It wasn't until several days later that he was able to share with my mother the horrible sight he had witnessed. During rescue work there is always the possibility of locating drowned bodies, however, on this day while flushing out a sewer he had come upon the body of a baby boy. My father, being a sensitive, loving man was emotionally overcome by this experience.

CHAPTER 5

▼

The term "housewife" was given to a woman who did not work outside of the home, which was the case of all the women of Hamilton Place. A woman's only priority was to take care of her house and children. The "housewives" of Hamilton Place followed a very strict work schedule. (I often thought the person who originated this schedule must have been a man!) My mother, being a very hard working woman followed this schedule to the letter.

Monday, was designated as laundry day. The essentials needed for washing clothes was a wringer washing machine (if you could afford one), a wash tub and a scrubbing board. Mother used brown cakes of soap which Dad brought home in wooden boxes. She shaved the cakes using a sharp knife into the hot water in the washing machine. Laundry soap in boxes was something we could not afford. During the summer, clothing was hung outside on clothes lines propped up with wooden poles to keep the clothes from dragging on the ground. Every back yard was filled with clothing flowing in the summer breeze. The children were banned from the back yard on Mondays.

The cleanliness of the clothing, the time of day in which you hung your first "load" and the way the clothes were hung was extremely important. Sheets must be washed and hung first since they were white and the wash water would be clean. My father's white shirts were washed second, followed by towels, then the colored clothing, slips, underwear, etc. in their own respective order. The heels of the socks must be turned the same way and, of course, in matched pairs. Again, this was all vitally important because there were sure to be watchful eyes peering from the windows, scrutinizing the laundry and the entire neighborhood would be informed of any discrepancies. You must be finished in time to start dinner and the clothes and clothesline must be taken down before dark. Anyone who left the clothesline hanging in the yard was considered lazy. Laundry day in the winter was less stressful since everything was hung in the kitchen. My brother, sisters and I played games hiding between the lines of clothing.

Tuesday was mending and ironing day. The clothes were sprinkled with water and rolled very tightly, placed into a wooden laundry basket and covered with a towel. I used to wonder why mother hung them out to dry, then wet them again only to iron them dry. When sufficient time had passed for the moisture to become well distributed throughout the rolls of clothing, the ironing process would begin.

They were called irons because they were made of heavy iron, square shaped on one end coming to a point on the other. The pointed end was to reach into small areas such as sleeve cuffs. Mother had two irons and one wooden handle. The iron portions were placed on the stove to heat. When one of the irons was hot enough mother would attach the wooden handle to the top and it was ready for ironing. When the first iron cooled, the wooden handle would be removed and the iron would be placed back on the stove to reheat. The second iron, which by now was hot would be attached to the wooden handle and was ready to be used for ironing. One iron was always on the stove being heated while Mother ironed with the second. This time consuming process was repeated over and over until all the clothes were ironed.

My father wore chef's hats which had to be very heavily starched. Mother ironed them until they were stiff enough to literally stand on the table. Father's white chef uniforms consisting of jackets and pants were also starched and ironed until very stiff. My two sisters, mother and I wore dresses every day which required ironing as well. I never saw my mother in slacks until I was thirty something. Hot summer days were made even hotter for mother when spent over those hot irons. When I became older I would be allowed to iron flat items such as tablecloths, pillowcases, and mother's cotton slips. By that time, with the grace of God and Westinghouse, we had an electric iron.

Our kitchen stove operated on coal. On the top of the stove there were small round holes in which iron lids were placed. The lids were removed by using an iron lid lifter. Pots were placed directly on the lids for cooking. Coal was placed inside the stove and the fire from the coal heated the stove lids. The oven also operated on coal. I often wondered today how my mother cooked all those delicious meals on that old iron stove with no visible way to lower or raise the heat. She must have been a genius!

Wednesday was the day for unfinished ironing, mending, or for special occasions; bread, rolls, cakes, etc. were fresh baked. Thursday was a day to do anything you didn't finish Monday, Tuesday or Wednesday.

When I was a little older my mother attempted to teach me how to darn my brother's socks. Johnny came home from school with a terrible limp and she became quite concerned. She thought of taking him to see Dr. Redinger, our family doctor, which involved taking two street cars to his office on Chestnut Street. After a little investigating she realized that I had darned the hole in the heel into a large lump which Johnny had been walking on the entire day. I believe it was at that time when mother decided being a seamstress would not be my calling in life.

Fridays the "upstairs" was cleaned and Saturday the "downstairs". Saturdays mother put soap all over the kitchen linoleum and scrubbed it over and over, rinsed it and then covered it with newspapers until it dried. This took half a day to accomplish. If you must go into the kitchen, "you better walk on those newspapers." Sunday was a "day of rest". The only chore mother did on Sunday was cook meals. If you followed this "schedule" to the letter, you were considered a "good housewife". If it rained on Monday, the entire "schedule" was moved up a day. Lord help you if you deviated from this "schedule" and hung clothes in the yard on a Tuesday! There most certainly would be questions asked!

Since no one in Hamilton Place had a checking account, one would travel to downtown Pittsburgh on the trolley (we referred to as a streetcar) going from place to place to pay bills and to shop. Only very wealthy people did business at a bank.

Downtown Pittsburgh was very busy with crowds of people everywhere. The street car would stop at the corner of Penn Avenue and Sixth Street one door away from the Roosevelt Hotel. Never having been inside of a hotel, nor imagining I ever would be, I was much in awe of the people going in and out. Taking the same route each time, we crossed Penn Avenue, walked past the Loew's Penn theater, then to Fifth Avenue, the busiest street in downtown Pittsburgh.

Anything you need could be found at Murphy's Five and Ten Cent Store on Fifth Avenue. After finishing our shopping in Murphy's, which took quite sometime, we would go to the very rear of the store where a huge meat market was located known as the Diamond Meat Market. In the morning the counters were filled with meat almost to the top and by the end of the day they would be empty.

A large assortment of meat consisting of brains, oxtails, short ribs, liver, lamb and just about any kind of meat imaginable could be found at the market. The fish counter had a large selection including but not restricted to items such as squid, snails, porgies, and smelts. There was a large counter filled to capacity with chicken as well.

Shopping at the Diamond Meat Market was not for sissies. The large crowd pushed and shoved one another to get the best cut of meat. If you were among the meek and didn't shout out your order very loudly, you might stand there all day and never be waited upon. The many workers behind the counters wore white aprons which, early in the day, were already stained with animal blood. This was the busiest place in downtown Pittsburgh.

Behind the meat market was an exit opening onto Market Place. The first building outside, along with many meat counters, also included just to the right upon entering, a long lunch counter known simply as "John's".It was here that my father was employed as a cook. The kitchen was located upstairs accessible only by climbing a wooden ladder attached to the wall. Food orders were shouted up to my father, he would prepare the plates of food and lower them into the waiting hands of the waitress by means of a "dumb waiter". Pans of dirty dishes were sent upstairs by the same means. When Mother and I stopped at "John's" to see my Father he would stick his head out of the window and wave to us. Sometimes we would sit at the counter and order a cold drink and Father would climb down the ladder to visit if he were not too busy. These trips are some of my favorite memories.

CHAPTER 6

▼

Looking back, I realize how simple life was. There was also a set of unwritten rules of conduct leaving little room for individual choices. This was our way of life, it was secure and predictable.

It was amazing how, in a place with no telephones, news traveled so quickly. There were no secrets. The connected walls held no protection from the eager ears of the neighbors. No conversation was private. Anything overheard was quickly spread throughout the neighborhood by the housewives who thrived on gossip.

The aroma of the different ethnic foods mingling together also spread quickly. At the first hint of dinners being prepared our stomachs would churn producing gastric juices and pangs of hunger. Those who could afford it had chicken for supper every Sunday. Mothers came to the doorways calling each of their children by name informing them that, "supper is ready". Meals were very simple and filling, with lots of potatoes and other starches.

Most children went to bed at precisely the same time. When the street light at the end of the rows came on which was the signal to head for home, children came running from everywhere. Mothers again came to the doorways, calling the names of the children who ignored the street light. One by one the names of the delinquent children were called to, "come inside and get ready for bed". If your name had to be called twice, you would be scolded. Within a few minutes, the cobblestone street would be empty.

Summers were very hot and winters were very cold with an abundance of snow. The rows of houses shaded the street from the sun, therefore, with the absence of snow plows and salt trucks, many years the cobblestones would not be visible until early spring.

The floor plan of each house was exactly the same; a kitchen and living room on the first floor, two small bedrooms and bathroom on the second floor and two rooms on the third floor, one of which was used for storage.

The kitchen floor was covered with linoleum, made in one piece. We kept the linoleum until the pattern was practically worn away. The replacing of new linoleum was a very exciting time. All the furniture was removed from the kitchen to make the job easier. We anxiously waited to see the new pattern on the floor, however after a few days we hardly noticed it. Neighbors were invited to admire the new linoleum.

Upon entering the house through the back door you stepped into the small kitchen. The iron stove was on the right, table and chairs in the center. Next to the stove were the green kitchen cupboard and the door to the cellar. On the left side was a deep stationary tub, which served the purpose of a kitchen sink and an icebox sat next to the tub. There was a large, deep pantry with shelves on three walls.

I can remember food being put into large bags and hung outside in the winter when the small icebox was either full or out of ice. This happened quite often since the iceman delivered ice on a very irregular basis. A placard provided by the iceman would be placed in the window with the number designating the pounds of ice you wished delivered facing the top.

The milkman delivered milk door to door in glass bottles. Since milk was not homogenized, the cream would rise to the top of the bottle. Once in a while, Mom and Dad would treat themselves to the luxury of using a little of the cream in their coffee. Most of the time however, the bottle would be shaken until the cream was distributed throughout the milk. In the winter months if the milk were not brought inside quickly enough the cream on top would freeze forcing the cardboard cap off the bottle and raising the cream approximately two and a half inches above the top of the bottle. This frozen cream was scooped from the top of the bottle and put aside to thaw.

The walls of the kitchen were painted, however, the walls of the bedrooms and living room were covered with wallpaper. When wallpaper needed replaced, the new paper was usually applied directly over the old paper. Some rooms had four, five or even six layers of paper on the walls.

When wallpaper was in need of cleaning, a thick pink substance that came in a can, called, appropriately, "wallpaper cleaner" was used. The entire family would be involved in the cleansing process. The small children would do the lower section of the wall and the older children would do the upper section using ladders, which were borrowed from neighbors. A small amount of the cleaner was rubbed on the wallpaper, which transferred the dirt to the cleaner. When the piece of cleaner turned black and began to harden it would be thrown away and a fresh piece taken from the can. This was a very time consuming process, therefore wallpaper was cleaned only when very dirty.

The cellar had a dirt floor and shelves on the walls where jars of fruit, tomatoes and other assorted vegetables that mother had "put up" in jars could be stored.

In a corner of the cellar stood a large white earthen crock or a wooden barrel in which sauerkraut was aging. Many heads of cabbage had been shredded, then placed in the large crock or barrel. Lots of salt had been added and the cabbage covered with water. A lid was placed on top and a large brick placed on top of the lid. Mother lifted the lid occasionally to make sure there was enough water to cover the kraut and she removed the salty brine (white residue) from the top. The tale tell aroma of the sauerkraut reached several houses away. This aging process took quite a long time. When mother announced that the aging process was completed, the rock and lid were lifted and the sauerkraut was ready to be consumed. To be completely honest, we children didn't really care if the sauerkraut was ever ready.

My two sisters Annetta and Helen slept in the second floor bedroom; my brother on the third floor. Since there was no other bed, I slept in a crib in my parent's room until I was nine years old. Father went to work very early in the morning making it necessary for him to go to bed at eight o'clock. I, being the youngest went to bed at the same time.

One of my fondest memories is lying in my father's bed snuggled up beside him looking into his strong face, listening to the stories he told. Sometimes he would read to me from the old bible written in Greek, an item he had brought with him when he left the St. Georges. My favorite story was of the Hebrew children called, "Shadrach, Meschach and Abendego".

The three children were told to bow down to King Nebakanezer. They refused, saying they would bow down only to their God in heaven. The king had them thrown into a fiery furnace. The king waited expecting to hear screams coming from the furnace, but instead, he heard singing. He commanded the soldiers to open the furnace door, whereupon the king saw an angel with wings spread over the children protecting them from the fire. Convinced that the God of the children must be greater than he, the king knelt down to the God of the children. I would request this story be read over and over.

I have not since felt as safe, warm, or secure as when I was lying in bed with my Dad's arms around me. The monsters and boogey men in the closet and under the bed were afraid to come out while my Dad was protecting me. After I fell asleep Dad would carry me to my crib.

No one owned a car in Hamilton Place. Men traveled to their jobs by streetcar, children walked to school. When I was old enough to venture away from our back yard I asked Mom to tell me when it was time for Dad to come home from work. Since there were no streets to be crossed on the way to the streetcar stop, Mom allowed me to walk the four blocks where I would sit on the curb and wait for my Dad. Sometimes I would wait for such a long time that the conductor's would feel sorry for me. They became used to seeing me wait there and often called to me saying, "He'll probably be on the next car".

When Dad stepped from the street car, I ran to him, hugged him and held his hand all the way home. I took his hat, climbed upon a chair and put it in the large round aluminum can kept on top of the green kitchen cupboard. Then I would take off his shoes, and put his slippers on his feet. I was certain there was no one in the whole world like my Dad. I continued to do this for many years, even after we moved from Hamilton Place, making a special point to meet him on rainy days carrying his large black umbrella that was almost as big as me, so he wouldn't get wet.

Occasionally, we would learn via the kid relay system that on a particular evening the city was to sponsor free movies on an outdoor screen. We gathered blankets and walked the eight blocks from our home to a large open area known as Fowler Field located close to the top of Charles Street. After the blankets were spread on the ground, we settled in waiting for the movie to begin. It was often a scary movie such as Frankenstein, Wolf Man or Dracula, an old musical or a Bud Abbott and Lou Costello movie. It was a warm night, many of the other neighborhood children would be there and we had great fun. I was four years old and often fell asleep very early in the movie lying on the blanket. My mother or brother Johnny carried me home.

CHAPTER 7

▼

I welcomed an opportunity to impress my older sisters since they considered me still a baby. Such an opportunity came unexpectedly one evening. Mom and Dad decided to make some root beer. Dad had bought all the ingredients, received instructions from a friend and set about making it.

Everyone had a designated job to do. Annetta and Helen washed the bottles with a long handled black brush and rinsed them very thoroughly. Dad was in charge of mixing the ingredients together. The root beer was put into the bottle using a funnel, and the bottle was placed on a "bottle capper". A metal bottle cap was placed on top of the bottle, then a handle was pulled down very hard, pressing the cap onto the bottle, sealing it. I was too little to pull the handle down so Annetta and Johnny had the privilege of performing the capping process. Helen and I were allowed to place the cap on top of the bottle.

When all the bottles were capped, they were taken to the cellar and placed on the narrow wooden shelves. Then the waiting began. I am sure our mother needed infinite patience to put up with our questioning every day as to the progress of the root beer. She would smile understandingly and patiently say, "not yet".

It was one evening after the root beer had been checked for the two hundredth time for drinking readiness. Everyone had gone to bed when mother called out to Annetta to "go downstairs and see if the cellar light had been turned off". Annetta cried back, "I am afraid to go downstairs, it is dark down there". Helen was then asked with the same reply. Johnny was on the third floor and couldn't hear mother's request. Here was my opportunity! I would prove to my sisters that I was no longer to be considered a baby. While mother was climbing out of bed to go downstairs, with much surprise to everyone, I called out, "I'm not afraid, I'll go down". I was hoping Mother would refuse my offer, however, to my disappointment, she agreed to let me go.

I climbed from my crib and stood at the top of the stairs. The stairwell to the first floor was very narrow enclosed with walls on both sides. I clung to these walls for dear life as I walked slowly one step at a time trying to ignore the strange creaky house noises heard only at night. I couldn't let my sisters know I was terrified; that would defeat the whole purpose of putting my life in danger this way. I reached the bottom of the stairs and stepped into the small hall area, turned to the left inching my way forward until I felt my bare toes touch the cold linoleum on the kitchen floor.

Oh no, the light switch was too high for me to reach! I hadn't counted on that! I would have to feel my way through the kitchen to the cellar door. I risked one hand by holding it into the kitchen to see if any of the ghosts, goblins or whatever comes out of the walls at night could see me. I brought my hand back in front of my face and it was still there intact, all five fingers. Maybe it would be all right to risk one leg. I slowly stepped into the kitchen and leaned against the wall. My eyes were still not accustomed to the dark, I could barely make out the outline of the kitchen table. I slowly felt my way along the wall stubbing my toe on the chair that stood in my path, kicking it away from the wall so I could pass behind it. I hid behind the chair for a few moments to gain courage and then continued feeling along the wall until I came to the cellar door.

At this point my internal dialog became overwhelming. What hideous sights awaited me behind that cellar door! I thought of running back upstairs and just telling Mom that the light had been turned off in the cellar. I thought of opening the door only to be met with the worst bunch of scary, slimy, crawly, green, gigantic, fang toothed, lizard skinned, monsters that a child could imagine. On the other hand, should I not open that door, who knows when another opportunity would arise to prove I was brave and worthy of my sisters' attention.

I could hear the growling of the monsters behind me. I was certain they were aware of my presence and were waiting to pull my arms and legs off at any second. I took a deep breath, reached out and felt my hand touch the knob on the cellar door. I turned it slightly to the right. With every last bit of courage a child of four could possess, I opened the door just a crack large enough to assure if there was light. Good, the monsters had not heard me. The cellar was entirely dark.

I am not sure whether or not I closed the cellar door or left it open, but no matter, I had accomplished what I had set out to do. This time I ran through the kitchen, into the small hall area, turned right and bounded up the stairs, bending down into a crawling position, my hands touching each step in front of me. My short legs had trouble keeping up with my hands. I could feel the long fingers of a large blue creature reaching out for my leg. I ran into my mother's room, jumped on her bed relaying the important information that nearly cost me my life. My sisters learned a new respect for me after that adventure.

CHAPTER 8

▼

It was an exciting time when a "huckster" came to Hamilton Place. Some had wooden, dilapidated trucks with large brown burlap sacks hanging from the sides containing potatoes, onions or other bulk items. They were cheerful hardworking men, their shirt sleeves rolled up nearly to their shoulders exposing huge muscles earned in their profession. Children came running from everywhere to see what the hucksters were selling. A few used the old trucks, but many had only a horse and wagon. Some sold produce, some fresh home baked pies, cakes, cookies and breakfast rolls. I loved the smell of the baker's truck. We practically pulled mother from the house when the baker's truck arrived. Frequently a man on foot, ringing a large bell to announce his arrival came into our neighborhood. He sharpened scissors and knives on a big rough wheel that was turned by pushing a pedal up and down with his foot. Yet another man who repaired umbrellas, rang a bell to attract attention and also arrived on foot.

The children's favorite was the iceball man who pushed a cart. We loved to watch as he shaved ice from a huge block, which was kept covered with a large heavy cloth to keep the ice from melting. He used a metal ice shaver, which looked pretty much like a planer used by carpenters except it caught the shaved ice inside. The top was opened and the shaved ice placed into a cone shaped paper cup. There were many large glass bottles filled with sweet, flavored, colored syrup. The iceball man would shake the bottles of syrup up and down over the paper cone until the ice was covered. A wooden spoon was stuck on top of the ice. I took the longest time of anyone to decide which flavor I wanted on my iceball. Was it to be banana, cherry, root beer, pineapple, orange or grape, or perhaps a combination of two different flavors? We gave up our nickels gladly to the iceball man. The wooden spoon always made me cringe when I put it in my mouth. On a particularly hot day, if you didn't eat very fast, you would have to drink the iceball.

As the horse drawn carts were leaving, the older boys including my brother Johnny ran behind singing their favorite song: "May-nure, May-nure is what the birdies eat, May-nure, May-nure gives the birds a treat, and if it wasn't for the May-nure all the little birds would die. Little piles of May-nure is what keeps the birds alive." It seems Mother was always scolding Johnny. It was this same group of older boys who gave Hamilton Place the nickname of "Hammy".

The garbage truck was our least favorite visitor to Hammy. Garbage was collected once a week or so, by men in open wooden trucks. Large pieces of smelly, dirty burlap hung from both sides of the trucks. The men spread the burlap on the ground, turned the garbage can upside down dumping the garbage onto the burlap. All four corners of the burlap would be brought together, lifted onto the garbage men's shoulders and they carried it up a flimsy ramp made out of a wide wooden board onto the truck. The ramp sagged and bent as they walked on it from the weight. The sack was then opened and the contents shaken onto an already huge pile of garbage. Garbage fell onto the street as the sack was picked up. The garbage men wouldn't pick anything up that fell from the sack or truck, therefore it would lie there smelling for quite a while attracting flies and neighbor's dogs until either it rained or someone would pick it up. The smell was worse during the summer months when the heat made it unbearable. This, of course, was before the invention of plastic bags and disposal trucks.

The garbage men's clothes and hands were filthy and reeked of garbage. When the truck became filled to capacity, it would be taken to a dump site, emptied and the men would continue their route. Although we were glad to have the garbage picked up, we hated to see the garbage men coming because the odor remained long after they had left.

At lunchtime the garbage men sat on a curb and ate sandwiches which they carried in paper bags. I wondered how they could eat their lunch with such dirty, smelly hands. Some of the children made fun of them saying that they were not paid very much but they were allowed to eat all of the garbage they wanted.

My mother was a very friendly, happy, God fearing woman and got along well with the other housewives. She had gained quite a few pounds since marrying my father. She was jolly, loved all the neighborhood children and enjoyed having a good time. She was one of the first to offer help to a family in need whether it be food, or just some emotional support.

Such a commotion on the street! Johnny and a few other boys came running home carrying a large brown burlap sack. It seems that a produce truck had struck a hole in the street and the bag of corn had fallen from the back. The boys chased the truck for several blocks trying to stop it to no avail. There were no telephones in Hamilton Place, therefor, when news needed to reach neighbors, the kid relay system was put into action. Mother sent the message around, and women came from everywhere. The corn was distributed to everyone according to the number of family members until it was depleted.

CHAPTER 9

▼

Another reason the hucksters were very welcome sights was because the closest store was Muellerschon's grocery store approximately five blocks from Hamilton Place.

Muellerschon's was a large grocery store with a wooden floor. Shelves stocked with all sorts of cans and boxes of groceries lined the four walls. Directly to the right as you entered the door was the biggest attraction of all: the largest penny candy display case I had ever seen. Some of the candy cost a penny each, however others you might get two or three pieces for a penny. Mrs. Muellerschon held a small paper bag in her hand and patiently waited until you made your choices. What an assortment they had! Little wax bottles with sweet colored water, black licorice hats and babies, Mary Janes, and at least a thousand more. On top of the candy counter were two large glass jars, one of which contained long salted pretzel sticks and the other held vanilla wafer cookies.

Since Muellerschon's was a gathering place, there were always many men sitting around discussing the problems of the world. In Mrs. Muellerschon's absence we shifted from foot to foot, trying to wait patiently until Mr. Muellerschon finished talking to the other men and noticed us standing there.

Even more than the penny candy counter, I loved the bakery in the storeroom in back. In the evening after the store was closed, Mr. Muellerschon baked donuts, crullers and lots of other indescribably delicious baked goods. On a breezy night, the wonderful, irresistible aroma of the fresh baked donuts found its way up Charles Street to Hamilton Place and points beyond. Then the pleading began. I have to admit that we didn't have to plead very long because mother enjoyed these treats just as much as we. Before long, with the money tight-fisted in his hand, Johnny, my two sisters and I walked down Charles Street to the bakery. Our feet moved quickly on these trips, unlike the walks to school, as our minds eye visualized and our mouths salivated, in anticipation.

If Mr. Muellerschon had a prosperous day in the store and was in a favorable mood, he opened the huge wooden back door of the storeroom where he did the baking and allow us inside to watch him stuff the donuts and crullers. He filled a tube with smooth white cream or jelly, then inserted the tip into the cruller or donut, filling them so full until the filling could be seen oozing out of both ends. On top he spread shiny chocolate icing. Watching him make the crullers was almost as enjoyable as eating them. Although these baked goods were to be sold in the store the next morning, Mr. Muellerschon allowed us to purchase some still warm from the oven.

His huge hands placed each cruller and donut so carefully in the cardboard box. This was indeed cruel and unusual punishment to make us wait a second longer. Mr. Muellerschon was a big man and always wore a white apron wrapped around his huge belly, tied in front with one small loop. I wondered if he was so huge from eating all the baked goods he made and I imagined myself with a huge belly. I didn't care, at that moment were I offered the riches of the world, I would have settled for just one of those wonderful cream filled crullers. The box was finally closed, the sides and top tucked inside and white string placed on all sides, tied with a bow on top. It seemed to take forever for this process and getting harder and harder to keep my legs and body still.

We walked very quickly, lovingly carrying the box, hoping the contents would remain warm until we reached our home. Still today, I dream of Muellerschons bakery and I am again biting into one of those magnificent crullers.

In order to reach Muellerschons Grocery Store, we had to pass through an area known at that time as "the colored section." This section began three blocks from Hamilton Place and continued to the end of Charles Street overflowing onto Brighton Road. I found this section interesting because it was very different than Hamilton Place. The cooking aromas were very different and the people would be sitting on the stoops. I often wondered why the "colored people" preferred to live in their own section! They always seemed happy and seldom noticed us as we passed by. If our eyes did meet we always smiled at them the way mother told us, and often someone would smile back.

There was one nasty girl however, who for some unknown reason, took an instant dislike to my sister Helen. When Helen walked by her house, she would come out with such a scowl on her face, push her into the street and begin to hit and punch her. We were sure she spent the entire day inside her house just waiting for Helen to come by. I would swing my arms at her, screaming and shouting, "you leave my sister alone", but I was much smaller and she paid no attention to me. I never understood why she hated Helen so much especially since Helen had never spoken to her. Finally, Helen managed to pull away from her and we ran the rest of the way home.

Helen made me promise not to tell mother, but she soon became too frightened and refused to go to the store. When mother questioned her as to the reason for not wanting to go, Helen would not answer. Without a satisfactory excuse mother thought Helen was simply being obstinate, therefor, she insisted that she go. Helen was so frightened, so I offered to go along. Maybe, if I screamed loud enough perhaps her mother or one of the people sitting on the stoops would make the colored girl stop. The time came when Helen became so frightened of this girl that we felt we had no choice except to walk into the woods that ran parallel to Charles Street in back of Hamilton Place. We followed the woods staying just inside, out of sight, until we reached a street named Strauss Street, below the area where the girl lived. We ran the rest of the way to Muellerschons. This worked for quite a while, however, we never told our Mother that we were going through the woods. I am not sure whether we were more afraid of walking through the woods or of the colored girl.

The people in the colored section never came to Hamilton Place, however once in a while one would pass by the entrance. We lived only a few blocks apart, yet it might as well have been a world apart, no one ever associated with the other. The only real contact I had with a colored person was the girl that beat up my sister, therefore, she was the only one on which I could base an opinion.

One day a few of the neighbor boys came running into Hamilton Place yelling to everyone that the "colored people" were coming to Hamilton Place that night to beat everyone with sticks and baseball bats. There was a lot of talking going on between the adults. All the children ran home screaming. I thought of the girl hitting Helen and I begged my Mom and Dad to lock all the doors and windows. After dinner I ran upstairs and hid under my mother's bed. I was sure someone was going to be killed. I worried about my brother, Johnny since he always seemed to be in the middle of everything.

What could have happened to make the colored people so angry at us? Why did they hate us so much? I lay under the bed for a long time listening for sounds of fighting, but none came. Mother finally convinced me to come out, that everything was alright, but I kept my head under the blanket for the rest of the night. I stayed in the house for several days.

Days later, I heard of an incident that had happened at the swimming pool on Cedar Avenue. I never heard all the details but apparently some white boys voiced their objections when a few colored boys came into the pool. Cedar Avenue was another section of the North-side far from Hamilton Place, therefore we could not understand what this had to do with our neighborhood?

I didn't go to Muellerschons for a while. After some time had passed and I again ventured down Charles Street I walked much faster when going through the "colored section" and I no longer smiled at the people. I did not feel comfortable walking through that section again and felt as though I were trespassing and was quite sure I wasn't welcome there.

CHAPTER 10

▼

Although money was scarce in Hamilton Place, our parents never gave the impression that we were worse or better off than anyone else, therefore we believed that everyone lived as we did, from payday to payday. Clothes were handed down from child to child and when the youngest had outgrown them, any buttons were cut off, saved in a jar, and the clothes were used for dust or scrub rags. Shoes were worn until they were beyond repair. When a hole appeared in the sole, several layers of cardboard were cut to fit the inside of the shoe. When father had enough money to buy a piece of leather, he cut a piece the size of the sole and nailed it to the bottom of the shoe. We could not afford to take our shoes to a shoemaker.

There was seldom anything to spare, yet when there was a death in Hamilton Place the neighbors quickly responded. Those that could afford it brought food to the bereaved family. Those who had no food to contribute either cleaned the house, did the laundry or simply visited the family offering emotional support.

Deceased loved ones were kept in the living room either lying on the couch or in a coffin. I even heard of a few who would be viewed sitting in a chair. Funeral parlors were out of the question.

There were also many happier occasions when neighbors gathered together. It was on a beautiful warm Monday, (of course) the laundry had been removed from the clothesline, but before mother took the clothesline from the poles she and father had a great idea. They hung some blankets over the line to make a huge makeshift tent. Then mother activated the kid relay system to invite all the families in our row to "bring whatever you're cooking on the stove and we'll have a picnic". Makeshift tables made from boards and wooden horses were set up and everyone brought whatever food they were preparing for dinner. Bowls, plates, pots and casseroles were lined up on the tables. I guess you could say, it was our version of an ethnic fair. Practically every family from our row came. What a wonderful assortment of food, and how deliciously different everything tasted.

One family was reluctant to come because the father was out of work and they thought their contribution would be too meager. Sensing this, mother went to the home and convinced them that everyone was invited with or without a food contribution. "There would be plenty of food for everyone". One meal served often in the neighborhood was a one pot meal called, "Green Beans and Potatoes". On good days, you might even find a piece of ham in the pot. The women were always so busy there was little time for socializing with one another, therefore this was a great opportunity to get the latest gossip, exchange recipes and just communicate and get to know one another.

After dinner, the children put on sun suits, turned on the garden hose and had a great time squirting each other until they were drenched and cooled. Later that evening after the children were put to bed we heard the sounds of squealing and giggling outside. Peeking from the window we saw the grown ups fully clothed, men and women alike, squirting each other with the hose. They were so wet that their clothing clung to their bodies. We giggled at the sight of our neighbors and especially my mother looking this way. They were having so much fun. Before leaving for their respective homes, the neighbors promised that they must get together again, soon. Yes, money was scarce, but good times were plentiful.

Dad had promised to bring ice cream home from work. Mother held supper off as long as she could and then told us to go ahead and eat. As the evening wore on, although my mother tried to hide it, she was becoming very worried. When bedtime came and Dad was still not home Mother told us to go to bed and she would wake us for the ice cream. I lay in my crib waiting to hear sounds of my Dad coming in the back door. I looked around the room and my eyes caught sight of the black cardigan sweater he always wore, hanging on a chair beside the bed. A feeling of dread came over my entire body, "what if my Dad never came home, he would never again wear that sweater"! I lay there, so full of fear that I could not sleep, but covered my eyes and sobbed quietly so Mother would not hear.

With the sound of the back door opening, and upon hearing his voice in the kitchen I began to cry even harder. This time the tears were of relief. Annetta and Helen were asleep, but Johnny ran down the stairs only to be disappointed. Dad had more important things on his mind this day than ice cream. I wanted to go downstairs and hold him so tight and never let him leave the house again but I couldn't move. I listened to the voices of my mother and father until I finally fell asleep. The next morning I saw the black suitcase on top of the green kitchen cupboard. Dad couldn't spend whatever money was left for ice cream.

I remember many times when the black suitcase would be on top of the green kitchen cupboard. During these times, while having dinner, my father would tell me to "look outside the window at the pretty bird." When I turned away to look he would put food from his plate onto mine.

I was a very thin little girl with blue eyes and long blonde hair that hung straight down my back and bangs on my forehead. When it was decided that we needed a hair cut, a chair would be placed on the back porch, a towel wrapped around our neck and with his barber scissors, Dad gave Helen, Annetta and I a haircut. The neighborhood kids came to watch and tease us. My haircut always looked like a "Dutch Boy" cut with straight bangs on my forehead and a straight blunt cut all the way around.

The weatherman had predicted a very hot afternoon, so Mother had another of her brilliant ideas. She would make popsicles for all the neighborhood children. She mixed the ingredients and poured it into ice cube trays. When they were frozen, she took them to the back porch and called to the children, "who wants a popsicle"? The squealing children came running. It was our job to line everyone up single file at the bottom of the steps. Once they had received their popsicle, they went down the steps on the other side of the porch. Everything went so well, Mother decided she would make popsicles for the children several times that summer in different flavors. She made cherry, banana or my favorite, chocolate. In time, children began coming from Charles Street knocking on the door inquiring whether or not she would be making popsicles that day. Mother couldn't keep the supply up to the demand.

My mother was an extremely good hearted person and the first to offer anything we had to someone in need. Jobs were scarce and many men could be seen wandering around looking for work. Mother never turned away a hungry person. I saw a man mother had just finished feeding, upon leaving, place an "X" on the bottom step of our porch with white chalk. Mother told me that this "X" is placed there to let the next homeless person know where to get something to eat. A portion of whatever she had on the stove cooking for our supper was given to the homeless person. They preferred to sit on the steps of the back porch to eat although Mother invited them to come inside.

These were the times when people were more trusting of one another. We seldom felt the need to lock our doors from our neighbors. Each person knew the names and faces of all the people, including the children living in Hamilton Place. If a strange face appeared in the neighborhood everyone became aware of it and did not hesitate to ask who they were. Neighbor looked after neighbor. It was not uncommon for one neighbor to scold another's child with never a thought of repercussions from the child's parents. On the contrary, the child would often be taken home by the neighbor and his actions reported to the parents. So it seemed this closeness held disadvantages for the children. You were very cautious about getting into trouble with so many eyes watching.

CHAPTER II

▼

Yes, many of the people of Hamilton Place were willing to share what little they had., Some of the sharing was welcome, but then again, with the houses all connected, some was not. One very vivid memory stands out of a most unwelcome sharing. Annetta and Helen awoke one morning itching and scratching with little bites all over their bodies. Their bed sheets were spotted with little drops of blood.

It seems that a new neighbor had recently moved in and brought with them some very unwelcome guests. The bedbugs spread through the neighborhood very rapidly. The young boys ran up and down the street chanting, "Bedbug Row, Bedbug Row".

Mother was devastated! One of the neighbors gave her some advice on how to handle this most unwelcome situation. She removed the mattress and leaned the bedsprings against the headboard (before box springs, all beds had open springs). Lighted candles were handed to each of us and we were instructed to move it back and forth very slowly under the bedsprings. Newspapers were placed under the springs. The fire of the candles killed the bedbugs and they would drop to the floor onto the newspaper. We were totally sickened as the dead bugs and melted wax fell onto the newspaper. We continued to do this for a very long time until no more bugs fell to the floor. The smell of the burning candles and the burning bugs was so strong that I became dizzy and Mother made me go downstairs.

This process was repeated several times over the next few weeks until mother was certain that there were no more bugs. The new neighbors were reported to the landlord who took prompt action. They were given a short amount of time to get rid of the bugs after which there would be an inspection. If they did not comply they would be forced to move from Hamilton Place. For several weeks the smell of burning candles seemed to be everywhere. After that experience when Mom bought candles, we were afraid we were sharing again with a neighbor.

CHAPTER 12

▼

Hamilton Place was a wonderful growing up place. One of our favorite past times was going to the summer matinee at the Brighton Theater located on Brighton Road. Mom gave us each ten cents, five cents for the ticket and the other five cents was for candy. When we needed money and the black suitcase was on top of the green cupboard we were left to our own resources. A sure-fire way of acquiring some money was to walk the neighborhood and empty lot picking up discarded pop bottles. These were taken to Muellerschon's where we were paid two cents return deposit for small bottles and five cents for the larger ones. After gathering as many friends together that could scrounge enough money, we began our trek the many blocks down Charles Street, past the Uniondale Cemetery, up the steep city steps onto Brighton Road. The Brighton Theater was approximately five blocks further down Brighton Road. Walking with a group made the trip seem much closer.

The show consisted of five or six cartoons along with a Laurel & Hardy or Abbott & Costello feature, a serial episode of Hopalong Cassidy or Flash Gordon, starring Buster Crabbe and his nemesis, Ming. Just as the hero was about to fall off a cliff or his rocket ship was about to crash into a mountain, words across the screen would inform us that the serial was "continued until next time". Children would cheer, shout, boo, run up and down the aisles making so much noise it might as well have been a silent film, for no one heard a word being spoken on the screen. Shoes stuck to the floor from spilled Coca Cola, popcorn and pretzels were everywhere, jujubees and gum were stuck under the seats and candy wrappers scattered all around. All in all, it was great fun and our favorite summer past time. Very few adults ventured into the summer matinees. The young ushers tried their best to keep order, but it was a losing battle.

Occasionally, on a Sunday evening, Mom took us hand in hand to the Brighton Theater. She especially enjoyed the musicals with Carmen Miranda, Mickey Rooney, Judy Garland, Dorothy Lamour, Esther Williams, John Payne, and so many others popular stars of the day. Clark Gable was her very favorite movie star. Halfway through designated movies the projector would stop, the lights would come on and a man would walk on stage holding a microphone. He announced that some lucky person was about to win a very special prize. A seat number was called and the winner received a set of dishes or glasses. On the way home we might stop at the drugstore soda fountain for a sundae or a soda. I usually picked a marshmallow sundae that cost eleven cents. I really like nuts on top, but they cost extra so I never asked for them.

A great way to occupy time, especially during the winter months was to have a collection of some sort. I was very proud of my Dixie Cup collection. Under the cardboard lid of a Dixie Cup ice cream container was the picture of a famous movie star taken from one of their latest movies. By removing the inner section of the lid and turning it over you could insert the picture. The outer lid served as a frame for the picture. I had the largest collection in the neighborhood because the bigger kids gave their lids to me. Doubles could be traded with other children for ones you didn't have.

Everyone collected comic books. For five cents you could purchase the latest issue of Superman, Tarzan, Captain Marvel, Wonder Woman, Batman, or my favorite, called Classic Comics, which were the classic books condensed in comic book form. These were our superheroes.

A boy living on Charles Street owned the largest assortment of comic books around and occasionally he was willing to swap. We were told that he was very ill and could not leave the house so collecting comic books was his hobby. This presented a problem since he lived next to the Uniondale Cemetery. There was always the usual horror story going around about a boy or girl who passed the cemetery at night and was never heard from again. It was difficult to find someone willing to go with you during the day and almost impossible to find someone to agree to go at night.

Those fortunate enough to have a comic book that he did not have, which was very rare, were permitted to enter his kitchen and peruse through his massive assortment. Sometimes it took quite a while to make a choice since there were boxes and boxes from which to choose. Since his collection was the largest around he had no any problem driving a hard bargain for the most popular issues asking for two or three books in exchange for one of the more popular issues.

Weddings were a most welcome sight in Hamilton Place because wedding receptions were held at the home of the bride. We sat in front of the bridal house prepared to wait all day if necessary waiting, listening to the music, watching the door. We knew eventually a member of the wedding party, usually the groom or best man, would come on the porch and throw coins into the street. Everyone scrambled over the ground picking up the coins. As one would imagine the older children managed to round up the coins while the younger children were pushed aside. I had enough of this, I was determined at this reception to do whatever necessary to get some coins!

When the groom appeared I steadied myself and after the melee was over, I opened my fist. To my amazement I had managed to collect seven coins in my hand. I couldn't wait to show mother and was starting for home when a colored boy approached me and asked to see how many coins I had. Although I was surprised to see him in Hamilton

Place, I was so proud of myself, at my accomplishment over the older larger children, I trustingly opened my hand. Quick as a flash he hit my hand from beneath throwing the coins into the air. Before I realized what was happening, he had scooped up the coins and ran away.

I screamed and cried, but only for a few moments when anger took over and I began running after him. I didn't think to look both ways as I crossed Charles Street and watched as he ran into one of the houses. Without hesitation I marched up the steps of the house fists clenched and knocked on the door. Boy, were his mother and father going to be angry at him! They surely would make him give me back my wedding coins!

As the door opened, I related the dirty deed to the man standing in the doorway, sobbing with every word. The man replied, "I will tell him to give them back", after which he closed the door. I stood on the stoop for quite sometime waiting for the boy to appear. After a while I knocked again and again but no one came to the door. I stood there in disbelief as I realized that the boy was not coming out! My first thought was to run home and tell my family. But, what if they came here, started shouting and everyone became angry? What if the man hit my brother or mother and father? What if my brother or father hit the man? Could the wedding coins cause a big fight between the colored people and the people of Hamilton Place? Is this what happened the first time? I ran as fast as my short legs would carry me back to my house and never spoke of the incident. It was then that I learned that not everyone could be trusted.

CHAPTER 13

▼

Mr. Lando of Lando Realtors was the owner of Hamilton Place. He was a man of Italian decent, with a slight stature, who always wore a dark suit, a necktie and dark hat. Each month Mr. Lando went door to door collecting the month's rent. As he approached Hamilton Place, word spread very quickly of his arrival. Children stopped their play to observe him while the adults went inside their homes. Doors began closing very quietly on the houses where fathers were out of work. Even his name brought frowns to the faces of our neighbors. He never spoke as he passed by making his rent collections.

Mr. Lando liked and trusted my mother so he offered her a job working for him as caretaker of Hamilton Place. When a family moved away, Mother's job was to check the empty house for damage and cleanliness and place a "For Rent" sign in the window. The keys were kept at our house so mother could show the houses to prospective lessees thus saving Mr. Lando many trips. For this work, we received a discount in our rent. The large "For Rent" signs were kept behind our big black leather sofa bed in the living room. The black sofa bed came in handy on many occasions.

From time to time nurses from the State Board of Health would visit some of the homes in the neighborhood. Doctors in the area would send them to visit homes where someone had been diagnosed with a contagious disease. After the nurses spent some time inside examining the patient they would hang a large white sign on the front door on which the word "Quarantined" was written in bright red letters. The sound of the nail being hammered into the door could be heard all over Hamilton Place. Everyone looked from the window to see on whose door the sign was being hung. No one was allowed to either enter or leave the house as long as the sign remained. The sign must be taken down only by the Board of Health nurse once it was determined that the person afflicted was no longer contagious.

The quarantine sign had been nailed to our door many times during my childhood. Mother had explained to us that the sign meant the illness was contagious but not necessarily serious. It warned outsiders to stay clear of the quarantined house to prevent the disease from spreading.

When someone in the house contacted a contagious disease the black leather sofa bed was opened allowing mother to separate the afflicted child from the rest of us. With all the precautions mother took, the disease eventually spread to every child in the family. Sometimes there would be two or three of us sleeping in the black leather sofa bed at the same time. Days passed very slowly on the black sofa bed. It was so boring just lying there listening to Mom's soap operas. She never missed an episode of Ma Perkins. Mother brought us food and coloring books or cut outs to keep us busy. If we had Chicken Pox she brought a large bottle of Calamine Lotion and dabbed it on each itching lump. We would point to each one pleading, "put some here". It didn't work for very long and when it dried, it left pinkish white spots all over the body. When a child had measles the blinds on the living room windows were pulled down in order to keep the room very dark. It was believed that bright light could damage the eyes.

When once again we were able to go to the kitchen for our meals, we were amazed at how different and bright everything seemed as though we had been away for a long time. When the sign was removed we flew outside as though we had just been released from a cage, anxious to see our friends again, sometimes only to find that their home too, had been quarantined. Often there would be signs on several houses at the same time.

Children often gaze into their parents' eyes for a sign in order to determine their own reaction to a situation. I saw concern in my mother's eyes that day. Surely, I thought, someone must be terribly ill or even dying. Johnny had scarlet fever. Even the name frightened me! This was more serious than the usual measles, chicken pox or mumps. The nurses came several times to examine him and gave mother medicine, which she administered to Johnny around the clock. The look of concern remained in my mother's eyes throughout the confinement, until Johnny was out of danger.

My beautiful brother Johnny was a typically active boy, always getting into some sort of mischief. Many times he came home from play with a broken arm. He broke his arms on five different occasions during his childhood; the left arm three times and the right arm twice. One break occurred while he was sled riding on Charles Street and he slid under a parked car catching his arm underneath. Johnny fell from a tree, breaking his arm the second time and still another while fighting with one of the other boys, the weakened arm became twisted and broke. Each time, mother would take him to the clinic at Allegheny General Hospital and bring him back with a cast on his arm. It seemed as though a cast were to be part of his permanent appearance. The doctor at the clinic told my mother should he break his left arm one more time it may become useless. There were also the usual inquiries from the school principal and child welfare.

I loved my brother very much. When my sisters, Helen and Annetta did not want their baby sister hanging around, Johnny would feel sorry for me and allow me to play with he and his friends. His friends were not always happy about this, but they knew better than to say anything about it.

I also loved my sisters very much. My sister Annetta, who was three years older than I had beautiful strawberry blond hair that fell in natural waves to her shoulders. Her skin was milky white while Helen and I were more olive toned. Helen was two years older than I and had beautiful dark thick, curly hair. She resembled my mother more than the rest of the children. I thought both of my sisters were quite beautiful. We were all thin with rosy red cheeks. Neighbors and friends would inquire of mother, "Hey, Tillie, what do you feed those children to give them such rosy red cheeks." Since Annetta and Helen had curly hair and mine was straight, mother explained that they must have run out of curly hair when they came to me.

CHAPTER 14

▼

Considering Dad's working hours and the distance we had to travel, we were able to attend church only on special occasions. We rode the #9 Charles Street streetcar to the intersection of East Ohio and Federal Streets. We then walked several blocks to Holy Trinity Greek Orthodox Church on Cedar Avenue. The streetcar fare was five cents for an adult and children under 12 rode free.

As we arrived in the vestibule of the church, the men greeted my Dad, they were so glad to see him. My father welcomed this opportunity to visit with many of his Grecian friends. They teased him because while he had dark hair, I was blonde with blue eyes, more characteristic of the northern Greeks. Mom took Annetta, Helen and Johnny with her inside while I stayed with my Dad clinging to his leg as I always did when we were away from home.

I enjoyed going to church, not only because the whole family went together and we wore our best clothes, but I also loved the beautiful pictures, the gold interior and the smell of the incense. Just inside the entrance of the Holy Trinity Greek Orthodox Church, there hung three beautiful icons of Jesus and our holy mother Mary, framed in glass. A large icon hung in the center with two smaller ones hanging on either side. People, upon entering the church approached the icons, blessing themselves with the sign of the cross and kissing one of them.

(Members of the Greek Orthodox faith cross themselves from their right shoulder to the left, the opposite of the Roman Catholic faith whose members cross from left to right). The grownups kissed the large icon and the children kissed the small ones hung lower so they could reach. My Dad held me up so I could kiss the large one. Eventually with all that kissing the glass became extremely smudged to the point that it was difficult to distinguish the face of Jesus and find a place with no lip imprints.

It was the custom in the Greek Orthodox Church that women and children sat on the left side of the church facing the altar while the men sat on the right side. Even though some of the men glanced at him disapprovingly, my father took me to sit with him on the right side. I sat very close leaning against his arm.

Having had no instruction in the Greek Orthodox faith, I had little understand of the meaning of the service. One of my favorite parts however, was when the priest proceeded down the aisle clad a beautiful maroon robe trimmed in gold, swinging a golden incense burner from side to side, the sweet smell of the incense filling the air around me. Another priest proceeded shortly after sprinkling holy water on everyone from a golden filigree wand. I sat up very straight hoping that some of the water would sprinkle upon me. After which seemed a very long service, we boarded the streetcar back to Hamilton Place.

Although we could not go to church every Sunday, we seldom missed the evening service on Good Friday and attended on Holy Saturday morning to receive Communion. After kissing one of the icons at the entrance, we proceeded to the left front side of the church where a priest would be standing with a beautiful gold and red cloth folded over his right arm. In his left hand he held a golden chalice containing wine and small pieces of bread. This he explained represented the body and blood of Christ. Alter boys stood off to the side of the priest holding golden trays on which lay large chunks of bread baked by the women of the church. The priest had blessed the bread, as well as the wine. We took our places in the single line of those receiving Holy

Communion. Using a tiny golden spoon in his right hand, the priest took a piece of the wine soaked bread from the golden chalice. Holding the gold and maroon cloth under your chin, he placed the spoon into your mouth. Then we ate a piece of bread taken from one of the gold trays.

I asked mother whether she thought it right for everyone to use the same spoon. Mother replied that no one ever got sick taking the wine from the same spoon because, "both the wine and the spoon have been blessed".

Every other year people of the Greek Orthodox faith celebrate Easter two weeks later than other religions. The in between year it is celebrated on the same day. Easter was a very special time at our house. We each received a basket with either a large hollow chocolate hen, rabbit or baby (our choice) in the center with colored hard boiled eggs, yellow marshmallow chicks and jelly beans sprinkled all around. Mother made Greek Easter bread with brightly colored hard-boiled eggs baked right on top of the bread. Of course, there was always lamb for Easter dinner.

My father taught me a game he used to play as a boy in Greece. While I held my brightly colored egg in an upright position, he hit the tip of my egg using the tip of his egg. If my egg broke, he won the game and was entitled to take my egg. I never won this game, but Dad never took my egg. He shared with me the secret of winning the game. He always used an egg with a pointed tip, then tap the tip of the egg on his front teeth. He said this was to make the egg stronger. I did this, but still never won.

Mom and Dad always did their very best to make the holidays special for us, especially Christmas, even when the black suitcase was on the green kitchen cupboard.

It was the custom everywhere that Christmas trees were never trimmed until Christmas Eve, and always done by Santa Claus. Dad always managed to provide a beautiful tree which Santa decorated with lots of shimmering icicles. Underneath the tree, however, was a different story. There was a large train, lions, guardhouses with soldiers standing guard and many cannons. It appeared more like an army base overrun with lions. Somehow it felt wrong to have symbols of war under a tree commemorating the birthday of the "Prince of Peace." I hoped that the baby Jesus would not mind and wished that one Christmas we could have something else under our tree.

On Christmas morning my two sisters and I would each find a new baby doll in a cardboard box leaning against the Christmas tree. We were permitted to play with this baby doll during the Christmas week, but after the holidays were over and the tree was taken down, the doll would be placed back in the box and taken to the attic. From the attic the doll that we received the previous Christmas would be brought downstairs. I suppose the rationale was, if there were a year when we could not afford a doll, we always had a new one from the year before waiting in the attic. Over the year we usually forgot what the doll in the attic looked like, so it was the same as a receiving a new doll.

During Christmas day, usually in the afternoon, neighborhood children went from house to house viewing one another's Christmas tree. We were made to feel welcome and seldom left without being given piece of candy or some sort of treat. I hoped that no one noticed the unusual display under our tree. Too often we would go to a neighbor's house that didn't have a Christmas tree.

It was Christmas Eve just after dark, Dad picked me up and carried me into the living room to "show you something very special". The blinds had been pulled down on our two front windows, which stood side by side. Through the blinds I could see two large round glowing red lights. Certainly, I thought, these were two piercing eyes belonged to none other than the devil himself. I clung to my father burying my face in his chest crying. Father told me that these were the eyes of Santa Claus who was watching to make sure I was a good little girl. When my crying continued even harder, he realized this had been a big mistake. He took me to the window, opened the blinds and showed me the two Christmas wreaths with red lighted candles. This was the first time I had seen lighted Christmas wreaths. As a matter of fact, they were the first in the neighborhood! Dad held me close until I was no longer afraid.

The following year, Dad took two narrow pieces of wood, one longer than the other, attaching them together to form a cross. He then drilled holes in the cross, painted it white, and put a string of Christmas lights through the holes. The cross was plugged into an electric socket and hung in the window. Many neighbors came to see the lighted cross in our window. This did not frighten me.

Halloween was not one of my favorite times of the year. Besides being a scary time for small impressionable children, I was haunted with the thought that, just maybe, there were real witches and goblins out there waiting for me. I didn't do very well at "nuts". Most children dressed in homemade costumes either of a ghost, a hobo, or a witch. Now and then a brave boy not afraid of the teasing would dress as a girl. We knocked on neighbors doors and when they were opened we shouted, "nuts".

My sisters and I were not permitted to go outside of Hamilton Place on Halloween. We did very poorly, for most neighbors could not afford to give anything away. One year my sisters and I knocked on every door in our neighborhood and upon our return home our bags contained only one piece of fudge and one walnut for all our efforts. My brother, being older, was permitted to go to the top of Charles Street and even onto Perrysville Avenue with his friends. He returned with a pillowcase bulging with goodies. The pillowcase would be emptied onto the kitchen table as Annetta, Helen and I stood wantonly gazing at the candy, bubble gum, homemade peanut brittle, popcorn balls and apples. This represented over a year's allowance.

On Halloween Eve the big boys played tricks on the neighbors. The doors of the houses being close to one another were a big advantage to them. The screen door on one house was opened and one end of a long piece of black string was tied to the handle. The other end of black string was tied to the screen door handle on the next door, keeping it closed. With this done, they would slam the open door shut causing a loud bang. The neighbor would come to the door and upon opening his door caused the door next door to bang shut. This continued until one of the neighbors realized what was happening and removed the string.

Other tricks they played was placing what was known as "stink bombs" on porches, ring the doorbell and run away hiding to watch "the fun", or exchanging porch furniture among the neighbors. The next morning, men would be seen carrying a chair or glider belonging to someone else looking for their own.

The younger children put a large button on a piece of string, tying the two ends of the string together. The button was placed in the center and the string was wound up tightly by swinging the button in a circle. When the button was tight enough, it was placed against a window and the ends of the string would be pulled. This made a very loud grinding sound against the windowpane of an unsuspecting neighbor.

Of course, there was the usual soaping of windows and doorbell ringing. Most of the people took these things in stride because they were silly pranks causing no personal or property damage. I didn't like Halloween very much in those days. I joined in on these tricks simply to go along with the other kids, but I never enjoyed it because I was always fearful at the prospect of being caught.

CHAPTER 15

▼

Dad came home from work one day with a wonderful surprise. I named the lamb Curly. Each day I took Curly to the hillside at the end of the row and while I sat on the ground, Curly nibbled on grass. It goes without saying how badly I was teased by the other children who followed me around singing, "Mary had a little lamb......". I decided to avoid this by taking Curly on the hillside early in the morning while they were still asleep. Curly's world was limited to the kitchen, the back porch and the hillside. I was totally responsible for his care including cleaning up after him, but I didn't mind this at all. I lay on the floor watching and petting him thinking I was the luckiest girl ever. I laughed when his hooves made clopping sounds on the linoleum. During the day Curly was tied on the back porch. I must have been doing a great job because in just a few months I was amazed at how Curly had outgrown the kitchen.

I awoke one morning and dressed hurriedly for our morning walk up on the hillside only to find he wasn't in the kitchen or tied on the porch. I became frantic and began searching everywhere. Mother came outside and explained that Curly was no longer here. He had grown too large to keep and my Dad had taken him to a farm where he would be happier with lots of other lambs. "Since Dad left for work so early", she stated, "he didn't want to wake me". I listened to her words trying very hard to absorb all she was saying, however, I didn't understand why they had not explained this to me the night before. She explained that Dad could not bear to see me heartbroken. Mother tried in vain to convince me that this was the best thing we could do for Curly. I spent the rest of the day in my room sobbing in my crib.

Greek families traditionally eat a lot of lamb, especially at Easter time. Since we seldom had a piece of meat large enough to roast, the family sat at the kitchen table anticipating our Easter lamb dinner. As I began to eat, my brother began to whisper, "I know what we're eating". I wondered why mother was giving Johnny such angry, threatening looks. Ignoring her, he continued humming under his breath looking at me with a knowing grin. What I was thinking had to be wrong, it could not be! Like a bolt of lightning I jumped up from my chair knocking it to the floor and let out a scream I am sure most of Hamilton Place must have heard. Mother tried to console me, attempting to convince me that Johnny was only teasing, but somehow I knew it was true. When I had eaten lamb in the past, it never occurred to my young mind that the two were one and the same, that the meat actually came from a lamb.

Mother decided it was best that she tell me the truth. The restaurant owner where Dad worked had purchased the baby lamb and asked him if he would take it home and fatten it up so he could serve it in the restaurant. If he did this, he promised to give Dad a piece of the meat. Johnny had overheard this conversation between my parents. He was severely reprimanded for his indiscretion. I couldn't believe that my parents could do something so terrible to me.

The next few days were torment. I loved my parents so much that I couldn't stay angry and finally forced myself to believe that it was all right, that my father would not have done this without a very good reason, he was just doing his best to feed his family. There was no way they could have told me the plan when he brought the lamb home.

Most of the time, my world consisted of Hamilton Place and the path to and from Muellerschon's Grocery, however, on occasion Dad and I would go to one of his favorite places. Under the circumstances, he thought it would be a good time for the two of us to spend the day together so we rode the #9 Charles Street streetcar to the intersection of Federal and East Ohio Streets to a most wonderful interesting large building called "The Northside Market House". I dearly loved our trips there together. The building was one large room containing many, many sizes and shapes of counters. These counters were either owned by immigrants or employed them, each selling their own specialty. Some counters were filled with meat, others with fish, still others with produce, baked goods or home made candy. All of your needs could be met at the North Side Market House. The vendors made a good living for it was always busy with crowds of people bustling around trying to pick the best piece of meat, or the freshest fish, or the largest loaf of bread. Your purchase was wrapped in brown paper and tied with string. Everything was paid for in cash, there were no credit cards.

Towards the back of the building, off to one side stood a lunch counter where, if you didn't mind waiting for a seat, one could buy a sandwich, a bowl of home made soup, a cold drink, a cup of coffee or an entire meal. My Dad knew many of these vendors so he would stop at each counter and visit, sometimes for quite a while. I stood beside him holding onto his hand listening as he spoke, wishing I could also speak the Greek language so I could understand what they were saying. The Market House was an extremely noisy place with men shouting back and forth in many different languages. The floor of the Market House was covered with sawdust. I would make drawings with my foot in the sawdust while my Dad visited with his friends. After he made his purchases, we would always stopped at the lunch counter.

The most enjoyable aspect of the Northside Market House was its smells. From the moment you entered through one of the many doors, you sensed many different aromas mingling together. Even the fish smelled good to me. All of it: the smells, the noise, the food, the ethnic languages, the vendors, the sawdust, but mostly the feelings all combining to make up the glamour that was the Northside Market House. I cherished these trips with my Dad and I loved him so much that the hurt and disappointment I had felt over Curly was completely forgotten.

CHAPTER 16

▼

It was the day I had anticipated for so long, the day I would begin my formal education, the day I was to start kindergarten! Mother and I walked to Linwood Elementary School, located just a few blocks from our home on the upper end of Charles Street. We went into the school office and mother officially registered me as a student. Then she did something I couldn't believe! We went into the kindergarten room and she actually left me there alone! This I hadn't counted on! I suppose I expected mother to stay with me all day. It never occurred to me that she would leave me there! I looked around at all the strange faces staring back at me. One boy was sticking his tongue out at me while another giggled. They didn't like me! I could tell! Is this what I had been looking forward to these many months? How had I allowed my parents to talk me into this? What where all those wonderful things they had told me about going to school? How had my sisters and brother survived? Again I listened and believed my internal dialog. The teacher tried everything, but I would not stop crying. Several of the other children were also crying, but the teacher managed to appease them with one thing or another and eventually they gave up. I, on the other hand, was not so easily fooled.

The principal sent a note to Johnny's teacher telling him to report immediately to the office. Johnny was sure he had done something wrong and took a very long time to arrive at the office. When he was instructed to go to the kindergarten room to take me home, he was relieved. Instead of he being in trouble, it was his baby sister. He was delighted at the thought of getting out of school for the day, however his delight was short lived.

As we walked into our house I immediately ran to my mother with out stretched arms. I was certain she would give me a big hug and tell me how sorry she was for leaving me all alone in that terrible place and I would never have to go back there again. To my amazement, mother showed no sympathy at all. On the contrary, after giving me quite a lecture, she took me by the hand and just as General Grant's troops marched into Richmond, she marched the two of us back to Linwood School. She would have none of this nonsense! There would be no more crying!

At that point, I realized that I had no recourse but to make the best of this situation. Whatever was to happen to me in this horrible place, would be on my mother's head.

I looked around the room and saw the other children busying themselves with a lot of interesting activities. There was a small playhouse with a few tables and chairs inside which offered a place of refuge. On one of the tables my eyes caught sight of several tin plates filled with brightly colored beads of different shapes and sizes and some black shoestrings. As I sat down on one of the chairs, Mrs. Ewer, the kindergarten teacher came into the playhouse, sat down beside me. Taking my hands in hers she began to teach me how to string the beads on the black shoestring. Oh well, since I had to be there anyway…! Maybe she wasn't so bad after all. Stringing beads and drawing pictures became my favorite activities in kindergarten.

On special occasions the children would form a circle and Mrs. Ewer brought a large glass jar with a lid containing cream inside. As she played the piano the jar was passed from child to child. We sang songs as each child in turn shook the jar as hard as they could. This was continued for what seemed a very long time and then something magic began to happen! The cream began to thicken and turn into butter! When Mrs. Ewer decided that it was ready, we gathered around her squealing with delight. She spread the butter on crackers and distributed one to each child. I thought this was the most delicious butter in the whole world. For those who didn't want the butter there was jelly for the cracker.

At naptime the children ran to one of the benches against the wall to lie down. Since there was not enough bench space for everyone, the unlucky ones were given a piece of newspaper to lie on the floor. Most of the children fell asleep quickly, others would just lie quietly for about an hour. We were not permitted to talk during naptime. I think this rest period was more for the Mrs. Ewer than it was for the children.

After a few days I began to speak to and get along well with the other children. My kindergarten days lasted only a few short months, however, because Mrs. Ewer gave me a reading readiness test and I was placed in first grade in mid semester.

My first grade teacher, Miss Apple was very thin with shoulder length light brown hair. One incident that stands out in my memory was the day Miss Apple was teaching the class the meaning of the words, "over" and "under". To demonstrate, she instructed me to climb on top of her desk and stand there facing the class. She instructed Charles, one of my classmates to crawl under her desk. Thus, she explained, "Mary is over the desk, and Charles is under the desk". When she felt all their little minds had absorbed this to her satisfaction, she instructed Charles to come out from under her desk and take his seat. As I began to climb down, Miss Apple said, "Mary, I want you to stay on top of the desk". While I remained standing there, confused and uncomfortable because everyone was staring at me, she remarked to the class, "I want you to take a good look at Mary", for someday she will invent something to make life easier for everyone". I was then allowed to climb down and take my seat. I never forgot Miss Apple, however, I never understood what I had done to deserve such a statement nor did I have a clue what it meant. I recalled those words so often throughout my life and I wonder, were Miss Apple here today would she be disappointed and feel that I had let her down?

For some reason, Miss Apple considered me her pet and when she needed a volunteer to help her after class I gladly rose my hand. I felt so special when she chose me to stay after school and clean her erasers. Standing outside on the fire escape I was instructed to hit the erasers together. Chalk dust flew everywhere, especially on my dress and shoes. The erasers must be hit together until all the chalk dust was gone. I began to question the rationale of everyone being so anxious to be chosen for this chore. I promised myself never to raise my hand again. After the erasers were finished to her satisfaction, Mrs. Ewer looked for a cloth to clean the blackboard. All she could find was a handkerchief and a pair of old silk stockings. I stood there in amazement! How could I possibly clean the blackboard with stockings and a handkerchief? I told her I had to go because my brother and sisters were waiting to walk me home.

Miss Apple told my parents she would give us her piano if we could find a way to get it to our home. I cannot recall how we accomplished this seemingly impossible feat, but one day the big black leather sofa bed was moved to the other side of the living room to make room for our piano.

We could not afford lessons for all three girls, therefore, Annetta, being the oldest, was chosen to take lessons and she was to teach Helen and I. Helen didn't seem interested and Annetta wasn't too anxious to have me for a pupil, but I sat beside her on the piano bench and watched her practice, singing along to the songs in her book. A particular favorite of mine was "Robin Hood". As I recall the words were "Robin Hood ho, he lived in the deepest woods, with all of his merry men, the forest was happy then, Robin Hood, ho,......" For the longest time, I thought "Robin" was his first name, "Hood", was his middle name and "ho" was his last name. I never learned how to play that piano very well, however, I was able to pick out tunes by ear by watching Annetta play.

Miss Apple was a little flighty, and a bit of an airhead, but very nice with infinite patience while Miss Hess, our music teacher was a very strict disciplinarian. She was in the process of grouping the children according to vocal ability by having each one sing the scales individually. I, being painfully shy, was terrified the day I was called on to sing solo. I coughed and held my throat telling her that I had a sore throat and was unable to sing. She informed me, while taping her hand with a ruler, that I would sing the scales the following day, by myself, or I would fail the entire music course. I loved music, but I was too shy to sing solo especially when I knew I could not reach the high notes. I just knew everyone would laugh at me!

I missed my dinner that evening due to my stomach being tied in knots and I had a terrible time falling asleep in anticipation of the following day. Children seldom shared these experiences with parents because most of the time, parents would agree with the teacher. We were taught that the teacher was always right. When I closed my eyes in bed that night, I kept seeing Miss Hess standing in front of me tapping a ruler in the palm of her hand telling me that I had failed the entire music course.

As God would have it, night became morning and after exhausting every trick ever attempted by children all over the free world to get out of attending school, (including holding my stomach and moaning pitifully, limping, and refusing to eat) Mother would not relent (unfortunately, she knew all the tricks). She didn't even fall for the most successful tried and true trick of holding a thermometer under warm water.

I walked to school lagging behind my brother and sisters, hoping against hope that by some divine intervention, I would not reach the school building that day. Perhaps a dog would run from one of the houses along the way and bite me so severely that I had to be taken to the Allegheny General Hospital for treatment and I would miss the entire day of school. Or, perhaps I would trip on a crack in the sidewalk and fall on my face, breaking my nose. Anything, anything to prevent me from entering the school building that day.

Where was the angel with wings outstretched saving the children from the fiery furnace? My guardian angel was nowhere to be found. The bell was ringing and there I was sitting in Miss Apple's classroom shaking, crying inside, preparing for the lions that surely were waiting to devour me the second period in Miss Hess's class. I heard none of Miss Apple's instructions during the first period class. Every cell in my brain was being used to plot a way out of going to my second period music class. The fear was becoming overwhelming. I had myself in such a frenzy that it would have been impossible for me to sing anyway. I would have done literally anything to prevent facing Miss Hess that day.

When the bell rang ending first period and the class began to form a line in the hall to walk to second period, I froze in my tracks. I must do something! I must do something! Only a miracle could save me now. Out of the corner of my eye I saw my miracle, the sign on the door to the girls' lavatory. Here would be my sanctuary. I told my classmate in line behind me that I felt sick and had to go to the bathroom. When Miss Apple wasn't looking I quickly slipped unseen into the girls' lavatory.

What was that noise in my chest? My heart was pounding as I entered the last stall in the back of the girls lavatory, locked the door and climbed on top of the toilet. I even realized that by standing on top of the toilet, my feet could not be seen from outside the stall. I couldn't believe I was doing this, but basic survival had taken over. I moved so quickly and methodically as though I had rehearsed every step. As frightened as I was, Miss Hess frightened me even more. When I heard the tardy bell ring, I realized I had no alternative. I would be standing on that toilet with my hands outstretched, fingers barely touching the wall on either side, keeping out the world, until the third period, maybe for the rest of my life.

I stood there not moving, barely breathing, for what seemed an eternity listening intently to the door of the girl's lavatory open and close as students and teachers entered and left, my heart beating faster with every sound. Once someone looked under the door, pulling on the handle, but finding it locked must have thought the toilet was out of order and left. I believe I actually stopped breathing at that moment.

When at last I heard the most welcome sound of the bell ending the second period, I quietly climbed down from the toilet, unlocked the door and peeked out into the world. Nothing had changed after my ordeal! Everything still looked the same! One more hurdle to go and I would be home free. I waited until I saw my classmates walking back single file to Miss Apple's room. When they were right beside the lavatory, hiding the door, I quickly stepped back in line in front of my classmate. She poured questions at me that went unanswered. Trying to quiet her before someone overheard her, but still afraid to hear her answer, I asked the big question, "had Miss Hess asked about me?" I held my breath awaiting her answer when she replied, "No, she hadn't". This, was the first and last time I ever cut class in my entire educational career. I was probably the youngest child in Linwood School, perhaps the entire world to "cut a class" in first grade.

I knew eventually I had to go back to Miss Hess's class. I prayed that this being a Friday, she would forget about me over the weekend. I suppose God smiled on me that day for when I returned to her class on Monday, there were no questions asked about my absence on Friday. I could not believe what my ears were not hearing! In fact, she was almost pleasant that day making me wonder what had happened to her over the weekend? After school I ran home and went straight to the picture on the wall in my mother's bedroom. The picture of two children crossing a rickety old bridge with wooden slats, some of which were falling into a tumultuous river below leaving gaping, open areas that the children, if they took the wrong step, would fall through. I closed my eyes and thanked the guardian angel looking over them, leading them safely across the bridge. I then decided that elementary school was certainly not for sissies.

The candy store across the street from Linwood School was the perfect place to unload the heavy burden of my ten cents a week allowance lying in my pocket. Or, we could walk to the largest selection of penny candy "in the world" at Muellerschon's Grocery Store. For five cents we could purchase a large bag of vanilla wafers, a bag of penny candy that would last for several days or a bottle of soda pop. We were the only children who actually received an allowance. Of course, we had assigned chores to earn this generous amount of money.

Located next door to Linwood Elementary School, was Annunciation Catholic School. Catholic Schools had the reputation of being much more strict on the students than the public schools. When a child misbehaved in a public school they were threatened by being told that either they mend their ways or they would be sent to a parochial school "where they won't put up with your nonsense". This was held over our heads as a form of impending punishment. It was believed that catholic school students never cursed or lied and were perfect children who would, when they died, most certainly go straight to heaven.

The students at Annunciation School wore uniforms and did not associate with the lowly Linwood protestant students. I avoided these children as much as possible because they always made me feel uncomfortable with their stares and whispers. This was my first experience with class distinction. It was a most unpleasant, degrading feeling.

A huge bell reverberated through the North Side of Pittsburgh summoning the Annunication students to school. I secretly wished I were one of those students who had the giant bell calling me to school each morning. When I finally mustered up the courage to speak to one of the Catholic students, they simply ignored me, probably wondering where I would get the idea that they could possibly want to associate with me.

CHAPTER 17

▼

Large machines began to appear in the large empty lot across the street from Linwood Elementary School. I overheard some of the older children saying that a swimming pool was to be built there. My second grade classroom overlooked the digging site and despite warnings from the teacher, many eyes would turn from the blackboard to the window when she was not looking. We watched the large hole being dug, then as weeks went by, concrete was being poured. After many weeks most of the students tired of watching, losing interest in the construction, beginning to think the swimming pool would never be finished. The workers became used to seeing me stop to watch them on the way home from school. They didn't even mind my question every week, "when can I come swimming"?

The weeks became months until I began to feel that summer would be here and gone before that pool would be finished. The time came when I noticed that gradually more and more of the heavy equipment began to leave the building site. On one of my daily passing, one of the workers shouted, "Hey, little girl, you can come swimming next week".

Only then did I realize, I didn't have a bathing suit! Mother would find a solution, she always did. After rummaging through many boxes in the attic she found an old bathing suit. It was black, made out of wool, with wide straps, a round neckline and the bottom came almost down to my knees. I hesitated, but just for a second, wrapped a towel around it and laid it beside my crib. I would be ready the day that pool opened. I am not sure where mother found suits for Annetta and Helen, but although theirs suits were also made of wool, they were very different from mine.

We kept our suits wrapped in towels ready to take to school the next day and every day until the day of the grand opening. We were among the first children to enter the building and to swim in Pleasant Valley Swimming Pool. I hadn't realized that my bathing suit would draw so much attention. Every time someone passed by, they pointed at me staring and laughing. I stayed under the water with just my head above so no one would see my suit. My sisters, brother and I went swimming almost daily at P.V. pool. Eventually mother was able to find a more modern bathing suits for me.

On Sundays, we walked home from P.V. pool a little faster than usual because we knew that every Sunday mother would be making our favorite dinner, Chicken with Macaroni. It was a Greek recipe Dad had taught to Mom. We could almost smell the tomatoes and garlic several blocks from Hamilton Place and our feet responded.

Mother had a dream one night that Johnny was walking down Charles Street. She could see his blonde curly head bobbing up and down above the wall surrounding Hamilton Place as he approached. He was coming home to tell her that I had drowned in PV pool. The dream frightened her to the point that she, believing it to be a premonition, did not allow me to go swimming for some time. Eventually, she rationalized the situation, and only with a promise from Johnny that he would stay right beside me was I allowed to go swimming again. Johnny was not too happy about this, so once we got to the pool I told him to go to the deep end with his friends and I would stay in the shallow end. He made me promise that I would not jump into the pool or go any deeper than my waist since I could not yet swim. This would be a day I was not to forget.

It was getting close to closing time and just about everyone had left the pool. This particular day Annetta and Helen had not come swimming. I was alone in the shallow section as I had promised and Johnny was with his friends in the deep end. A young boy about Johnny's age swam close by and began talking to me. He said I was such a pretty girl and he wanted to teach me how to swim. I wanted to learn to swim very badly so I could go in the deep end with my brother and sisters. I told him I would like to learn to swim. He reached down touching my hand and asked me if I would like a Popsicle. Of course, I replied that I would. So very quickly, he put his hand up the leg of my bathing suit and was touching me. I had no understanding of what was happening, but I felt very uncomfortable and tried to walk away. He held onto my hand and continued talking, saying things that I did not understand. He asked me to put my hand inside his swimsuit. He said if I did this, he would buy me a Popsicle. Mother had never covered this situation, so I knew nothing about what was going on, but I did not want to do what he asked. I said "No" pushing him away and began to cause quite a commotion splashing the water and yelling. When I called to my brother Johnny, the boy quickly got out of the pool and went into the boys locker room.

I climbed out of the pool and ran to the deep end calling for Johnny. I told him what had happened and he and his friends ran into the locker room searching for the boy. He never told me what happened in the locker room but Johnny never left me alone again. I promised not to tell mother because I knew she would be angry at him for leaving me alone.

The cement at the bottom of P.V. pool was so rough that after swimming for a few days, the bottom of our feet looked as tough they had been sliced with a razor blade. The cuts were superficial, not deep enough to bleed but our feet still hurt. Even this did not deter us, as we enjoyed the coolness and fun of the pool more than we minded the cuts on our feet. We all agreed not to show mother because she might not let us swim anymore. I enjoyed swimming at Pleasant Valley Pool for many years, proudly stating to everyone, "I was there the first day it opened".

CHAPTER 18

▼

When we were not swimming at P.V. pool or at the movies, summer days in Hamilton Place were spent playing games outside on the white cobblestone street. When mother used the last of the Quaker oatmeal, we took turns to decide who would be given the empty box. There seemed to be no end to the things you could do with an empty oatmeal box. By covering it with colored construction paper we had a pretty container for our crayons or other treasures, or with a small pair of scissors, make a doll house, cradle, install wheels and it became a truck or car. You were limited to the things you could make or the games you could play only by the size of your imagination.

My favorite toy was a Raggedy Ann doll I received for my birthday. She was soft and cuddly, kept me safe at night and was my constant companion.

Dad made us a swing for the back yard. It was very sturdy with five metal poles and had a very heavy chain with large links. Dad made us promise that we would share it with everyone. All of the neighborhood kids came to take turns riding the swing. It was determined that a "turn" was the length of time it took to sing any song that the person swinging would choose. Everyone tried to think of the longest song that they knew with many verses so that their turn would last longer. Often I became nauseated and had to give up my turn. We spent many, many hours swinging and singing with our neighborhood friends.

Many times we coaxed Dad to put up the makeshift tent in the back yard. My two sisters and I decided it would be fun to put on shows for the other kids. At first, we just sang and danced or recited poetry. Later, we began to act out children's stories such as Hansel and Gretel. We wanted to charge everyone a penny to see the play but mother objected saying that there may be children who didn't have a penny and that wouldn't be fair. So, we compromised, and without her knowledge, we charged a button or safety pin, certain that everyone must have a button around the house. This seemed like a good idea until I saw a boy tear a button from his shirt to pay his admission. After several performances we presented our mother with a jar full of buttons and safety pins. She was not pleased with this idea either, so we were told to give back the buttons and safety pins. We began to give everyone who came to see the play a button or safety pin, their choice. Once the jar was empty, the plays were free.

Many of the children wanted to take part in the plays so we would frequently enlist the help of other children when we had extra parts. The plays became very popular and the children would encourage us by requesting more and more.

We entertained ourselves playing games such as: Run Sheep Run, Kick the Can, Buck Buck, How Many Fingers up? Release, Hide and Seek, Stick Ball. One day while playing Hide and Seek, as I was hiding one of the boys crept up behind me and as I turned around he gave me a kiss on the check. After I recovered from the shock, I ran home to tell my sisters. They thought I was a terrible person to let a boy kiss me. For a while I felt guilty, as though I had done something wrong, thinking I was a very bad person because I really liked it. I think what I really wanted to do was to brag to my sisters that a boy had actually kissed their little sister, so there! That was my very first kiss.

On rainy days we played "Hide and Seek" in the house. The one who was "it" would wait downstairs while the rest hid upstairs. This day, Johnny was "it". My sisters took great joy in finding small obscure place in which to hide me where I couldn't be found. Since I was so small they had limitless choices.

This day they chose a piece of furniture on the third floor known as a "dry sink". It had two drawers on the left side, and a door on the right side opening into a small empty space. Annetta and Helen shoved me into the small empty space, closed the door and left to hide themselves. It was very dark inside with the door closed and I was extremely cramped. For a while, I was delighted because I was sure Johnny, wouldn't find me.

After much time went by, I began to wonder what would happen if he didn't find me; or perhaps my sisters had forgotten where they had hidden me. I tried very hard to open the door with no success and I began to cry and call out. No one heard me! Annetta and Helen had been "found", the game had ended and everyone was downstairs. They had entirely forgotten about me enclosed in that small piece of furniture.

Eventually mother asked about me and they became frantic. They ran up the stairs to the third floor and flung open the door of the dry sink. I was crying very hard by then and very angry at them for forgetting me. They made me promise never to tell our mother what had happened. If mother only knew of the numerous times we made promises to one another not to tell her of things we had done!

CHAPTER 19

▼

Was it really true? Did I really have another sister and brother? Mom and Dad gathered us together around the kitchen table for a family discussion. Mom told us that we had another sister and brother who would be coming to live with us. That was just about all the information we were given, just as much as we needed to know. There had been a lot of whispering going on between Dad and Mom for quite some time with the kitchen door closed.

I was six years old, too young or just to overcome with joy to think of the obvious questions. Just the thought of having a new sister and brother seemed wonderful! The fact that they were coming to live with us was even more wonderful! In years to come I would have many questions, and the answers would all be revealed to me, but for now all I needed or cared to know was that I had another sister and brother. Sarah & Eugene's last name was King. Even this did not bring questions to my mind. The only question that needed answered as far as I was concerned was, "How soon will they be here?"

Mother began to prepare the house for their arrival. Eugene would sleep in the attic bedroom with Johnny while Sarah would share the small bedroom with Annetta and Helen. They would be very crowded, but it would have to do. Mom planned a special supper for the day of their arrival, she was happier than I had ever seen her. Her children were coming home at last!

I immediately began to make plans of my own. I must have some sort of present to give my new brother and sister when they arrived to make them feel welcome. I had spent all of my ten cents allowance, so I had to think of something else to give them. I tore a page from my favorite coloring book and colored it for Eugene, being very careful not to go outside of the lines. I was so proud of that picture and couldn't wait to give it to him. He would think I was such an artist! The only thing I had to give Sarah was my new pencil.

On the morning of the arrival, Mother was very nervous as she prepared for this, the big day. Before she left, she told us the approximate time she expected to return. She had no sooner closed the door than I began to watch the clock. As the big hand and little hand approached the expected time of arrival, I ran to the kitchen window and stood watching the pathway in the lower section of the yard waiting, waiting. Clutching the colored picture in one hand and the pencil in the other, my eyes were focused on the opening in the cement wall, afraid to look away for fear that, for certain, they would arrive at that moment.

Suddenly there they were! Mother was coming through the opening, with her was a young girl of 16 and a boy of 14. Even though he had a frightened look on his face, I thought I had never seen a more beautiful boy. He had curly blonde hair, and looked surprisingly like my brother Johnny. Even this did not raise questions in my young mind after all, they were both my brothers! Although a very pretty girl, Sarah was very thin with dark hair and very pale skin. On her face was a look of apprehension, and she was obviously very timid and withdrawn. She lacked the rosy cheeks, which were the Theodore family trademark. My eyes followed the trio as they came up the stairs, onto the porch, into the kitchen and into my life. They were really here! I immediately loved them.

Eugene and Sarah stood quietly in the kitchen. Mother said to Annetta, Helen, Johnny and I, "This is your sister, Sarah, and your brother, Eugene". We each mumbled a quiet, "Hello". I took this opportunity to hand the picture to Eugene, saying "I colored this for you". He looked at me with anger on his face and said only "behave". I didn't understand! Didn't he see how happy I was to see him? I handed the pencil to Sarah, she took it and said politely, "Thank You". Not knowing the circumstances I could not understand why they both seemed so angry. Were they angry at me? Maybe Eugene didn't like the picture. Maybe I should have used more blue on the sky? I hadn't gone outside of the lines! They took their bags of clothing upstairs where they stayed until supper was ready. It had never occurred to me that they would not be as happy to see me as I was to see them.

CHAPTER 20

▼

Mother never spoke of her life before meeting my father. It was from bits and pieces acquired over the years that I learned of Mother's previous marriage and the hardships she had to endure as a child.

Mother lived on a farm with thirteen brothers and sisters, when times were extremely hard for everyone and very few children had the luxury of going to school further than the fifth or sixth grade. Although they earned only pennies a day, it was necessary for the children to find a job as soon as possible to assist the family. As soon as Mother finished the sixth grade, her parents sent her to live and work in a cigar factory with many other girls her age.

The girls slept in a large room with two rows of beds. They were given very few possessions: a bed to sleep in and two nightgowns, which they were responsible to keep clean. All other clothing was to be provided by their parents and all wages they earned were sent directly to their parents.

When mother was eighteen years old, she left the cigar factory. Her parents tried to persuade her to return, but mother refused. For the next three years she worked at various jobs and continued to send money to her family until at age 21, she met a young man. John King made her feel important and beautiful and convinced her that he would take care of her. After too brief of a time, she consented to marry him. She dreamed the dream of so many young girls, to have children of her own, a home in which she could be safe and secure with a man who loved her.

For the first few years Mathilda and John were very happy. Although life was a struggle for everyone at the time, they managed to purchase a small house and lived a relatively good life.

Their first born was a son named John who was born prematurely and lived only thirteen days. Then mother gave birth to a baby girl who was "still born". Their third child Alfred was a healthy, little boy.

Alfred often made trips to the grocery store for people in the neighborhood. At age seven, while on one of these trips, he slipped from the sidewalk and fell into the path of a truck. He lived for only a short time and eventually died of congestive heart failure, known at the time as "Dropsy." A daughter, Sarah Jane was born on May 20, 1923 and another son, Eugene Howard was born on December 23, 1925.

Although he had a loving wife and a beautiful son and daughter, after the death of Alfred, John King began to change dramatically. He was no longer the happy loving man Mathilda had married. He began to drink heavily, stopping each payday at the nearest bar and did not return home until his entire week's wages were gone. When they were on the verge of losing their home, John King could no longer handle the enormity of the situation and the family fell apart. He left his wife during her sixth pregnancy with two children to feed.

There were times when the only food in the house was a potato that Eugene had begged from a neighbor. Mother's sister, Marie came to visit and found her lying on the floor, pregnant and very ill with malnutrition. Mother was immediately hospitalized, leaving no one to care for Eugene and Sarah who were sent to live at Juvenile Court. Mother remained in the hospital until she gave birth to my half brother, which she named Paul Allen. His Godfather eventually changed his name to John Paul. Johnny? My half brother? Johnny was not my whole brother? He had lived with us all of his life! But, it was true, Johnny's birth name was King.

When Mother and infant son were released from the hospital they were sent to the "fresh air camp" where met Anthony Theodore.

Shortly after Sarah and Eugene moved in with us, Johnny was told the circumstances of his birth. My father always thought of Johnny as his son and he was the only father Johnny had known. Since John King had not been seen nor heard from since before Johnny's birth, it was always my father's wish to someday legally adopt Johnny. Adoption papers had been prepared, however, before they could be finalized, Johnny made a startling announcement. For reasons unknown, perhaps only stubbornness, or maybe as a means of bonding with Eugene, he wished his name to remain John Paul King. No amount of talking would change his mind.

As he grew older, there would be many arguments between Dad, Mother and Johnny over this issue. Adoption papers were rescinded and Johnny would forever be known as John Paul King. My parents were heartbroken over his decision. Throughout the years, they tried several times to change his mind with no success.

CHAPTER 21

▼

As time passed, Sarah began to feel more comfortable with her new surroundings and family. Eugene however, remained quiet and was easily upset for quite some time. As was planned, Sarah shared the bedroom with Annetta and Helen while Eugene slept on the third floor bedroom with Johnny. I was still in the crib in my parent's bedroom. Each time I tried to speak to Eugene, he would simply say, "behave" in a dismissing manner. We did not dare enter the sanctity of the third floor bedroom. This was strictly off limits to the girls.

Eugene and Johnny became very close and soon were inseparable. On rainy days they would play cards on the front porch with their friends. At times, they let me play cards with them, but only if they were short a player. My brothers taught me how to play Pinochle and Five Hundred. Eventually with mother's constant reassurance, Eugene's anger subsided as he came to realize that here, perhaps he could feel safe and finally at home.

Sarah was put in charge when mother went to downtown Pittsburgh on the streetcar to pay bills and shop. Mother shopped at Murphy's 5 & 10 cents store located on Fifth Avenue where she could find almost anything she needed. On these days Sarah would make soup for lunch from a package (similar to Lipton) called, "Minute Man Chicken Noodle Soup" It was called "Minute Man" because it "takes only a minute to cook it". I thought this was the most delicious soup I had ever eaten. Every time mom went to town this was my lunch request. I thought my sister had to be the best cook ever! I had a very warm feeling towards Sarah from the day I first saw her. She seemed so sad much of the time.

When it was introduced to the public I mailed a post card to the address on the radio and was the first in our neighborhood to sample Ovaltine. Jergens Lotion was also a new product on the market from whom we received samples as well.

Sarah was offered a job with a family who needed a live-in mother's helper. She would be there all week and come home only on an occasional Sunday. I missed my sister very much. I looked forward to Sundays and would sit on the curb at the streetcar stop, this time waiting for my sister to come home. Once in a while she would be carrying a small white paper bag with delicious chocolate chip cookies that we would share on the way home. Sarah introduced me to my first chocolate chip cookies.

Sarah had a streetcar pass that was good at any time. There was a streetcar that provided transportation from the top of Charles Street and continued down to Muellerschon's Grocery Store. It would remain there for a short time, at which time the conductor got off the streetcar, reversed a pulley that connected the car to the electric cable overhead, remove the steering wheel and carry it to the other end of the car. After connecting the steering wheel on the opposite end, it was possible for the streetcar to reverse and travel in the opposite direction up Charles Street to Perrysville Avenue. This car was referred to as the "Dinky". The back of the seats reversed so you could ride either facing backwards or forwards.

On Sundays, when there was nothing else to do, Sarah loaned Annetta, Helen and I her weekly streetcar pass. Annetta was the first to get on the Dinky, show the conductor the pass, take a seat and slip the pass through the window to Helen. Helen boarded, showed the pass to the conductor, and slipped it through the window to me. We three rode the "Dinky" up and down Charles Street for hours. I am sure the conductor caught on but since there were few people riding on a Sunday, I suppose he didn't mind. As a matter of fact, we provided a welcome break in the boredom of driving an empty streetcar up and down the same street all day.

CHAPTER 22

▼

One of the neighborhood boys bought a sling shooter. Not everyone could afford to buy one so most of the boys being very inventive, including my brothers, made one using a piece of a tree branch. The branch had to be from a section of the tree that formed the letter "Y" where two branches came together. A thick band of 1 or 1 ½ inch wide rubber was also needed. The ends of the rubber band were cut thinner at both ends and tied to either ends of the Y. A "hossle" (very tiny crab apple) was placed in the center of the rubber band. The process involved holding on to the "hossle" and pulling back on the rubber band with one hand, holding tight to the bottom end of the Y with the other hand. When you let go of the rubber band, the "hossle" was projected a pretty far distance. Although this model was much different than the one David used to slew Goliath, it was the same concept.

This proved to be a very dangerous toy as several of the children began using stones instead of the softer "hossles". Mothers began noticing unexplained bruises. One boy was taken to the clinic at Allegheny General Hospital from being struck in the eye, and birds and squirrels were being shot out of trees on the hillside, the sling shooters became a thing of the past.

I still can't (or won't) explain how that navy bean got inside of my ear. After the demise of the sling shooter the children turned to the bean shooter. A bean shooter was simply a small cylindrical tube much like a paper straw into which a navy bean was inserted. By blowing into one end, the navy bean flew out of the other end. The boys chose sides and had bean shooter fights.

My ear had been hurting since afternoon. Mother looked inside by pulling the top out and holding a flashlight over it. Imagine her surprise! Somehow a navy bean had lodged pretty far down in my ear and try as she may, she could not remove it. Mother held onto my arm, rather tightly, as we sat in the waiting room of Allegheny General Hospital clinic. I am sure this trip had not fit into her plans for the day. Her state of irritation was increased by the many hours we had to wait to see a doctor. The doctor listened to mother's diagnosis, examined my ear, and shaking his head back and forth with a worried look on his face made a startling statement. If he failed to retrieve the bean it would eventually begin to grow. I would soon have a bean sprout coming out of my ear. After all, he was a doctor, so I believed him. I looked at Mother for reassurance, but saw only a look of annoyance.

I sat there crying at the thought of having a bean sprout growing out of my ear, and wondering "where in the world was Jack and his famous magical bean stock chopping axe when I needed him"? Mother held my head still and I hardly felt a thing as the doctor reached into my ear with a long pair of tweezers and dislodged the bean quite easily. What a relief when I saw that bean in the tweezers! As you might guess, bean shooters were also considered dangerous and were banned from Hamilton Place.

Unlike John King, my father was not a drinking man. The only liquor to be found in our home was an occasional bottle of ouzo father kept in the pantry. Ouzo is made with anise and is a common drink among the people of Greece. The Greeks also refer to it as Annisette, or sometimes Dad called it Moustika. On cold mornings he would put a little in his coffee to keep himself warm on the way to work.

Mother decided to surprise father with a party in honor of his "name day", (St. Anthony's Day). Due to the size of our house, she could invite only a few of his friends and one or two close neighbors. This was probably the first party he had ever had in his entire life. I loved seeing my father so happy. Mother had managed to buy a few bottles of ouzo and kept them hidden from him.

As the bottles of ouzo were emptied in the living room, they were brought to the kitchen to be thrown away. There was a little ouzo left in the bottom of each bottle which Johnny immediately decided was meant for him to drink. He emptied each bottle into a small glass and try as we might, Eugene, Anetta, Helen and I could not talk him out of it. He lifted the glass to his lips and without a second thought of the consequences Johnny promptly drained the glass dry.

We four stood there amazed that he did not drop over dead. It wasn't very long, however before he began to act strange, giggling and talking very funny. Eugene decided it was in the best interest of everyone to get Johnny upstairs and into bed before Mom or Dad could see him. With our combined effort we managed to get him up the two flights of stairs into the bedroom. The following morning Johnny awoke very sick, holding his head and moaning. Mom and Dad managed to piece together the whole story and I never saw them so angry. We all received a severe tongue lashing, and finger shaking, however, all the scolding in the world could not punish Johnny as much as the headache and sick feeling he was experiencing from his first taste of alcohol.

CHAPTER 23

▼

Many of mother's family still lived in McKeesport, Pennsylvania, just southeast of Pittsburgh. With the absence of telephones, mother's only means of communication with her family was by mail. Among my mother's sisters, Aunt Marie was my favorite. She had blood curly hair, was very beautiful and always seemed to be happy. People said she reminded them of Penny Singleton of the Dagwood Bumstead movies. Aunt Marie didn't wear house dresses like my mom. She wore pretty skirts and blouses or ruffled dresses and she smelled so good. I so much wanted to be like my Aunt Marie.

I knew that mother and Aunt Marie were very close. I think the main reason that I liked her so much was because she always made my mother laugh. They would sit together telling each other stories, drinking coffee and laughing most of the afternoon. We were always happy to see Aunt Marie come for a visit. Once I overheard mother say that I reminded her of Marie and she had wanted to name me after her. Years later, my Aunt Marie would shoot and kill herself with a shotgun from complications brought about by "change of life".

Aunt Clara was another of my mother's sisters. She had married a short round Italian man named Sam Domingo who was a very happy, jolly man successful in his work. I liked him very much, except when he would sit in my Dad's black leather chair. Uncle Sam always wore a suit, a white shirt, tie and vest. Aunt Clara was a large woman who wore lots of perfume and fancy printed dresses. Aunt Clara intimidated many people including myself because she spoke in a very loud voice and had a hearty laugh. When Aunt Clara and Uncle Sam left, our home seemed very quiet.

Aunt Florence was the quietest of my mother's sisters, who visited us more often than the others. When she and mother would sit and talk they did not laugh but spoke in soft whispers. Aunt Florence gave the impression of being an unhappy, serious minded person.

A young man always accompanied her on these visits who was introduced as Aunt Florence's nephew, Arthur, whom we were to refer to as Cousin Arthur. He was always well dressed in a suit, white shirt and a necktie and worked in an office in downtown Pittsburgh. When he spoke of his job, he referred to as his "office", a term used only by people who had a very important position. He smoked lots of cigarettes, often smelled of liquor and was the first man I ever saw cross his legs when he sat down. Cousin Arthur seldom paid attention to us and I thought of him as well educated because he used a lot of words I didn't understand. The two lived together at the top of the incline in Mount Washington. When the truth was revealed we learned that Arthur was really Aunt Florence's son, a secret that would be kept by the family and unknown to Arthur for many years.

We visited them only on rare occasions because it meant riding a streetcar to downtown Pittsburgh, then the fare to ride the incline to Mt. Washington and a long walk to their home. Mother, Aunt Florence and Cousin Arthur always spoke in whispers when we were near.

Mother also had three brothers: Herman, who lived in McKeesport; Harry, who had moved to California and Frank, who settled in El Paso, Texas. I saw my three uncles only on two or three occasions throughout my life.

Aunt Marie had been married several times. She and her current husband owned a chicken farm which they had decided to sell. The chickens were brought to our house so that my father could "dress" them. When I heard this expression I couldn't wait to see the chickens in little suits and hats.

Our kitchen was very small and with three people and dozens of chickens, there wasn't much space for working. Several large pots were placed on the stove for boiling water. We were instructed to stay out of the kitchen. Mom, Dad and Aunt Marie set about chopping off the heads of the chickens, placing them in the large sink until all the blood drained out and then dropping them in the boiling water. The boiling water made the task of removing the feathers much easier. So, this was what was meant by "dressing" the chickens. Among the laughing coming from the kitchen there appeared such a racket that I opened the kitchen door just a bit and peeked in. Bad timing, for just at that time, a chicken ran past the door without a head. It had slipped from my father's hands and landed on the floor. The chicken was actually running around the kitchen without a head! Blood was being splattered everywhere. Mother and Aunt Marie were laughing and trying to catch the chicken. I began to scream whereupon Mother saw me and quickly closed the door.

Once the chickens were all "dressed" they set about the huge task of cleaning the kitchen. The chickens were bundled up in brown paper and Aunt Marie took them home. Every time I hear the expression, "running around like a chicken with it's head cut off", I recall my first hand experience.

CHAPTER 24

▼

It was a chilly December afternoon, the smell of our usual Sunday dinner of chicken and macaroni filling the kitchen. My mother was in the kitchen crying while listening to the radio. President Franklin Delano Roosevelt, whom my mother loved and respected, was speaking. We heard the words, "a day that will live in infamy." Mother was crying for all the young men who had been killed in the bombing of Pearl Harbor. The entire family gathered around the radio listening to the President's words informing everyone that the Japanese had "without provocation" bombed Pearl Harbor. Thousands of American sailors and civilians had been killed by this "dastardly attack". Life, as we knew it, would never again be the same.

When a catastrophic or important incident occurred, an extra newspaper would be printed immediately in order to inform the public. This newspaper would be given to newsboys who ran through the streets of the city shouting, "Extra, extra, read all about it." People everywhere came from their homes to buy a copy of this special edition.

The following day President Roosevelt would declare that a state of war existed between the United States of America and the Empire of Japan. These words began the beginning of World War II which would last almost four years. Although many of the words were hard for me to comprehend, as our president spoke, I saw the look of fear on my parents' faces. I knew this was a fear far greater than that which I felt while hiding in the girls' room in first grade or checking the light in the basement. I was eight years old and my thoughts were of bombs falling on Hamilton Place. No one could foresee the impact these words would have on the entire world, perhaps with the exception of the men in whose minds burning memories of World War I still lie smoldering. It was indeed a day unlike any other in the history of our country.

My mother along with most Americans had a special fondness for President Franklin Delano Roosevelt. It was not uncommon to see his picture, such as the one hanging in our living room, proudly displayed in homes everywhere. Mother thought he was the greatest man of our time, and the only man she considered being worthy of her vote. She expressed her faith and confidence in President Roosevelt as she stated, with anger and determination in her voice, "he will pull the country together and make short work of this war". Her fear seemed to diminish as she spoke of her confidence in our President and our country.

The Draft Board immediately sprung into action. One by one young men were called to serve in the armed forces in defense of our country. Eugene and Johnny were still too young for the draft. Soon white banners with bright red borders, and gold cords and fringes began appearing in neighbor's windows. If the banners bore a blue star in the center this signified a young man in the family was serving in the armed forces. Many banners had two stars and still others had three or more. A gold star meant a young man had lost his life for his country. In these cases, the family received a telegram from the president, which would be delivered by a young boy on a bicycle.

Everyone searched desperately for a way to help our boys overseas. We were about to witness the real meaning of patriotism and sacrificing that spread over the entire country. All thoughts of the "old country" vanished, as immigrants stood ready and willing to defend their new country. No sacrifice would be too great for our service men.

Housewives saved the grease from frying pans in empty soup or vegetable cans, to be sent to factories for the manufacturing of ammunition. Children collected newspapers and cans. Nothing was thrown away that might be useful in the war effort.

Government ration books were distributed according to the number of persons in the family. It was decided that one day a week no one would eat meat in order to conserve it for our servicemen. "Meatless Tuesday" was being observed everywhere. Silk stockings were impossible to buy since the silk was used to make parachutes. Items such as meat, butter, sugar and many other items began disappearing from grocer's shelves. These and other items were rationed by the government. When purchasing a rationed item you must surrender a matching stamp from your ration book. You were chastised by; "Don't you know there's a war on", when attempting to purchase a product on the rationed list.

Although the fence was still standing, Mr. Barnett put aside his feelings and sponsored a group of children into the "Junior Commandos". Annetta, Helen and I were one of the firsts to join. We were very proud to say we were Junior Commandos. We wore a green armband with two pieces of black elastic that held it onto the upper portion of our arm, bearing the words, "Junior Commando" printed in white letters to all meetings.

Our job was to collect tin cans and all the scrap iron we could find. When the school day ended we ran home, put on our armbands and went door to door collecting cans. We searched the empty lots and the neighboring hillsides. Both lids were cut from the cans, placed inside, then flattened by stomping on it with our shoes. The Barnett family had large piles of cans and scrap iron in their back yard. Yes, we were actually allowed to enter their back yard! I supposed they considered this their sacrifice for the war effort. When the piles became too large, a truck was called for pickup. Mother was very annoyed when our shoes began to wear so quickly since they were also on the list of scarce items. Mr. Barnett was told to find other means of flattening the tin cans.

"Uncle Sam", a fictitious character appeared on posters everywhere. He was a tall, very thin character with a long white beard, dressed in red, white and blue even to his high top hat. He was depicted as if he were pointing his finger at you and bore the caption, "Uncle Sam Needs You". Uncle Sam would be seen leading parades and appeared at all patriotic gatherings. Songs were written about him and he became the symbol of American patriotism.

I felt proud to think that I was in some small way contributing to help win the war. Never before had patriotism and love of country been so strong among all Americans. We listened nightly to the news broadcasts. Later, in 1943 Eugene would enlist in the Navy, however when Johnny became of age and attempted to enlist he was declared "4F", which meant he received a deferment and not acceptable due to a medical problem. In 1945 he would be accepted in the Merchant Marines.

Children seldom played in the street since spare time was spent helping the war effort. Many movie stars were enlisting in the armed services: Jimmy Stewart, Clark Gable, George Montgomery and so many others. A big majority of the movies being made were about the war. We kept abreast of the war from the radio every evening and special newsreels shown in the movie theaters. The most famous war correspondent of the time was Ernie Pyle, who I believe was the first to write newspaper and magazine articles directly from the front lines.

Our school began selling war bonds and stamps. Stamps were sold in ten and twenty five cent denominations. Every week mother gave us a dime or quarter to buy a stamp, which she pasted in her book. It took many weeks, but how proud we were when the book was filled and we could turn it in for a war bond. It was our patriotic duty to buy as many war bonds as we could afford.

"Any bonds today, bonds of freedom, that's what we're selling, any bonds to day...... ", were the words to a very popular song heard everywhere recorded by Frances Langford. Children and adults alike could be heard singing and humming the tune. It was a together time, for the entire country.

Families were informed to install black blinds in all windows, which must be pulled down during an air raid alert. This prevented a light from being seen by enemy planes. The stores could not keep up with the demand for black blinds. A loud siren signaled the beginning of an air raid at which time all lights must be turned off. If a light could be seen from one of your windows, a neighbor designated as the Air Raid Warden knocked on your door and warned you to "turn it off". He wore a simple uniform consisting of a round tin hat and brown jacket, and carried a flashlight. A very dim light was permitted inside as long as it was not visible from the street. During an air raid we listened intently for enemy planes overhead. A loud siren sounded the "all clear".

If there were an advance notice, air raids were a great opportunity for the young girls and boys to have "air raid parties". Plans were made ahead to be sure you were sitting next to a special boy when the lights were out.

CHAPTER 25

▼

There was a lot of commotion in the front street. Looking through the window I saw Sarah kissing Buzz Bickart, a neighborhood soldier who had just arrived home on leave. They were standing right in the middle of the front street. Sarah received a terrible talking to that day for, in mother's words, "making a spectacle of yourself in front the entire neighborhood!" "And what will everyone think of you?" Mother believed you should never do anything to draw attention.

Unnecessary talking was not permitted at the supper table by the children. We sat very quietly listening to mother and father's conversations. Mother was telling father that two soldiers known as M.Ps. (military police) were seen going in the big house in back looking for the young soldier who lived there with his parents. Apparently he was A.W.O.L. (absent without orders of leave). "When they catch him", mother informed father, "they will throw his ass in jail".

Now, as a child with a very vivid imagination and as some would say, a keen sense of humor, I sat there imagining what a person would look like without an ass. I often told funny stories to the other children and was always given the part of the funny character in all our plays. The more I pictured this, the funnier it seemed. Without first sending the words by way of the brain to consider the consequences, I blurted out, "What will they do with the rest of him?"

Were there an Olympic medal for quickness of hand, mother would be wearing the gold that day. In less than an instant, her hand flew across my mouth. For the first time I regretted having the honor of sitting beside mother at the supper table. I put my head down so my sisters and brother would not see me crying.

After supper was over and the children left the room, I heard mother and father laughing in the kitchen. This took a little of the sting from my face to know that my humor had not gone entirely unappreciated. They considered my remark disrespectful, and according to the standards of the day, I probably deserved to be disciplined, however I caught myself smiling at the prospect that the humor had not escaped them.

You would expect that this first small attempt at humor would have cured me for life, but it had little impact. On the contrary, hearing the laughter from my first audience, however small, was encouraging. It felt good to make people laugh!

CHAPTER 26

▼

In the midst of all the war effort, something totally awesome was about to happen. A new neighbor moved into Hamilton Place! To everyone's amazement, history was about to be made. The first colored person was moving into our neighborhood, and only two houses away from ours! It was a woman who lived alone! This was the most exciting thing that had happened in Hamilton Place. My imagination went wild with questions! Were all the houses in the colored section full? Why didn't she want to live there? I always thought that the colored people wanted to live together, that this is the way it was meant to be. Why was she moving into an area where there were only white people? Were the other colored people angry with her? Mother could not deal with all my questions.

Suddenly, talk of World War II took a temporary back seat to this new neighbor who became the topic of conversation. Several neighbors swore to move immediately and some actually began looking for a different house to rent. My thoughts were of the girl on Charles Street that always hit my sister Helen and the boy who took my wedding coins.

Since the children from the lower section of Charles Street attended Columbus Elementary School, these few encounters were the only basis on which I could form an opinion of colored people. The nasty comments I overheard from the neighbors combined with my past experiences gave me much anxiety. Yet, when in the vicinity of #5 Hamilton Place, for some reason I slowed my pace, hoping to get a glimpse of the colored lady.

One afternoon while playing in the back yard, I saw her appear on her back porch. With the usual curiosity of a child, I slowly began to bounce my ball closer to her house in order to get a better look. She was a very large woman with light brown skin, a round face and wore a housedress much like the other housewives of Hamilton Place. She was looking straight at me and she was smiling! I quickly turned my head away pretending I had not seen her, and began to walk away.

The strangest thing happened, I turned and looked back at her. Maybe it was because she had such a beautiful smile. She called out, "Hello, I'm Mrs. Clark". I stood there, frozen in place, staring at her, afraid to speak. "What's your name" she asked? I mumbled very quietly, "Mary". Then I quickly turned and ran home.

Running into the kitchen I shouted excitedly, "the colored lady spoke to me", whereupon mother asked what she had said. "She told me her name was Mrs. Clark and she asked my name", I replied! Mother, without out stopping her ironing, calmly asked, "Did you tell her your name". I was totally bewildered that mother showed absolutely no concern at this unprecedented news. "Yes", I answered, "and she smiled at me"! "That was nice", mother said. I was absolutely amazed! Mother had me totally confused! She was so calm and didn't seem to care that I had spoken to Mrs. Clark, even with all the horrible things everyone was saying! She hadn't told me to stay away from Mrs. Clark as the other parents had told their children. Why then, would I expect her to be concerned? All of this was too much for me to deal with. I went to sit on the front steps to think this over.

The following day, I again bounced my ball near Mrs. Clark's house. She came to the door and said, "Hello, Mary", again with that beautiful smile. I walked just a bit closer to her porch and replied, "Hello". She continued talking and I walked a bit closer. Then she totally confounded me by inviting me into her house! Now what do I do, what would mother say to this? I was very hesitant to enter her house for I had never been inside a colored person's home. I tried to think of an excuse not to go, but I didn't want to hurt Mrs. Clark's feelings. She seemed so nice, so I walked up her steps and stepped into her kitchen.

I was almost disappointed! I was not sure what I had expected to see, but it looked very much like the other kitchens in the row. A stove, refrigerator, table and chairs, nothing unusual! As I stood there just inside the door, Mrs. Clark asked if I would like a glass of water. She then began to do the most amazing thing I had ever seen. She removed a large jar of what appeared to be Vaseline Petroleum Jelly from a shelf. She took a handful of the jelly and began to rub it through her hair. Mrs. Clark further amazed me by picking up a strange looking long metal rod that had a wooden handle, and placed it on the stove. She explained that this rod was called a straightening iron. Heating the iron until it was very hot she began to roll her hair in the iron. I could not believe what happened next! Smoke began coming from Mrs. Clark's hair! I was sure her head was burning and I screamed, "Mrs. Clark, your head is on fire". Mrs. Clark tilted her head back and let out a hearty laugh. I had never heard anyone laugh quite like that. She assured me that she was not on fire, and explained that this was the way colored folks straightened their hair. Then we laughed together and I knew that Mrs. Clark and I would be friends. The combination of the Vaseline and smoking hair filled the room with a very strange, rather unpleasant odor. Even so, I watched in amazement while Mrs. Clark finished straightening her hair. She patiently answered my simple, perhaps even bordering on stupid questions.

Mrs. Clark was a very warm, friendly person not too unlike my mother and I enjoyed being with her. I began to visit Mrs. Clark quite frequently. Earlene Garvey had moved away a year before and Mrs. Clark was a welcome replacement. My mother was worried that I would become a pest, but Mrs. Clark always seemed happy to see me.

Since she lived alone, when she needed groceries, she gave me a list and I went to Muellerschon's Grocery Store for her. Mrs. Clark's pronunciation of some words made it difficult for me to understand all that she said, but I enjoyed listening to her. She became very sad when she spoke of her husband who had died a few years before. She missed him very much. I couldn't understand why some of the neighbors were saying such awful things about Mrs. Clark for she was a very likeable person. Although the neighbors criticized my mother for allowing me to spend so much time with Mrs. Clark, she ignored them saying that neither she or my father objected to Mrs. Clark.

CHAPTER 27

▼

Mother had secretly been saving small amounts of money for many years! No one, including my Dad was aware of this. It was obvious that we needed more room since Sarah and Eugene had come to live with us and I had long since outgrown the crib. Mother had been hoping to save enough money for a down payment on our very own house. When she felt she enough money saved, she decided the time had come to reveal this news to my Dad. As she spoke, we watched the expression on his face. Even though he could not find words, his eyes revealed the depth of his pride and appreciation for what my mother had done. It was almost an impossibility to save even a few cents with times as they were, yet she had done it! She had enough saved that they could begin the search for a house.

The following months my mother was very busy house hunting. She looked at so many houses, we began to feel that there was none to be found that we could afford. During supper mother described every minute detail of the houses she had seen that day. We sat quietly envisioning the house, absorbing every word. She spoke of a house not too far away located directly across from a public park with a swimming pool where we could play everyday. We could sense the excitement in her voice each time she spoke of our very own house. We all hoped that this would be the one she chose, but, it was not to be and the search continued.

Mother returned tired from house hunting one day to announce that she had found the perfect house and it was within our means. The family quickly gathered around the kitchen table and was given a detailed description. We listened intently as mother described the large dining room, living room with space for the piano, a bedroom so large that there would be enough room for all four girls. I was finally going to share a room with my sisters and sleep in a regular bed. NO MORE CRIB.

She went on to describe two more bedrooms on the second floor, two attic rooms and a small room that could be used as a sewing room. From my past experiences with sewing, I did not feel I would be spending much time in that room. The finished basement consisted of two rooms, one of which held a very large coal bin, the second had a laundry in one corner with ample space for a playroom. There was even built in shelves where our toys could be kept. We all agreed this house sounded perfect and was definitely worth waiting for. It was a large corner house at number thirty three Geranium Street. We would even have two numbers in our address! We must really be getting up in the world!

Johnny and Eugene made up a story that there was money hidden somewhere behind the unused fireplace in the living room. Annetta, Helen and I decided our first order of business would be to search every inch of the fireplace until we found that money. We went so far as to make plans on how we would spend it. Mother soon straightened us out on this point and my brothers was disciplined. We did not actually see the house until the day we moved in, except for the picture we carried in our minds from mother's description.

Where would we start? How could we possibly get all of our belongings from this house into the new one? Once again, the questions were posed to Mother. Could we take all of our toys? Are there any children in the neighborhood? The excitement was almost too much for us and I am sure it was for mother.

In time, as if by magic, everything was packed into boxes, bags or would be carried in our arms. The neighbors came by one by one, crying and hugging my Mother, telling her how much she would be missed. It was at these times that I almost hoped she would change her mind.

CHAPTER 28

▼

We moved from Hamilton Place in 1942, when I was nine years old. I left too young to be aware of how my life would forever be influenced by the people and the good times I had experienced there. I would never forget the people of Hamilton Place, for I was taking with me something special from each of them. I would miss my friends, the games, the plays, the smells of the ethnic cooking, the crullers from Muellerschon's Grocery Store, Linwood School, the hossle fights and so many things that combined, would determine what I was to become.

I said good-bye to my friends turning back only once as we rode away in the rented truck, too excited to understand that a big part of me was being left behind. Mrs. Clark had cried when I told her we were leaving. I cried too, for I knew I was losing a very good friend.

Many wonderful memories awaited me in the new house and the new neighborhood where I would spend the remainder of my childhood. Where, in the fifth grade I would meet Barbara Ann Means, who would remain my best friend for over 60 years. The place where I would live until I married in 1951, but my roots were in Hamilton Place, which would always hold a special place in my heart.

CHAPTER 29

Although over the years Eugene never spoke of the horrible experiences he and Sarah had endured, it was many years later that Sarah could bring herself to share those days with me.

When our mother was hospitalized, she and Eugene were made "wards of the court". They were taken to live at a special place for children known as Juvenile Court. Sarah assumed the role of protector for her younger brother since Eugene was quite young and not very strong. She told me of the time when Eugene became very ill. Sarah sat on the floor outside of his room listening intently as the doctor and nurse discussed his condition, continually knocking on the door shouting, "I want to see my brother". It was many days before Eugene began to recover and she was allowed to go inside to see him, however, Sarah continued her vigil in the hall outside and could not be moved until he was well.

Sarah and Eugene were placed in thirteen different foster homes in the following seven years. In some of which they suffered humiliating and degrading experiences far beyond what any child should have to endure.

Sarah's body began to tremble as she spoke of the day when, in one foster home, Eugene had been locked in the chicken coop as punishment for not finishing his supper. Sarah could hear him screaming in terror as the chickens pecked his head and body. She ran to open the door of the coop but the chickens were all around, pecking at her and Eugene. Pulling the door with all her strength, she finally managed to force it open, whereupon, she fell to the ground. Eugene ran from the coop with his blonde curly hair streaked with blood. Sarah tried to get up to chase the chickens away from him but her legs were bleeding and hurting. Eugene continued running with the chickens flying after him. Sarah finally got to her feet and ran after him shooing the chickens away as best she could. She knew she was in big trouble for letting the chickens out of the coop. It was a horrible experience that caused Sarah and Eugene to have nightmares for quite some time.

In this same foster home, Sarah slept in a very small room that was part of a long hallway which lead to two other bedrooms and a bathroom. Her room was only large enough to hold a very small bed. A young woman and a little girl slept in a large room next to her. At the other end of the hall was the grandfather's bedroom.

While lying in her bed one evening, Sarah heard the door at the other end of the hall open very quietly. Although the door to her room was closed she could hear footsteps creaking the wooden floor, slowly coming down the hall approaching her room. She saw the light of the hall stream in and heard music being played downstairs as her door was opened. A figure, which she recognized as the grandfather, quietly entered her room. He approached her bed, stood there for a moment, then leaned over and began rubbing his private parts across her body. Sarah screamed causing him to hurriedly run back down the hall to his room pretending to be asleep.

When Sarah, sobbing and hysterical, told the couple what had happened they did not believe her. They said she was lying and if she screamed again, they would lock her in the chicken coop. Even though this incident was repeated several times, they still would not believe her.

Sarah lay in bed night after night with her eyes tightly closed in fear, hoping that the old man would believe her to be asleep and would not bother her. One night Sarah awoke with the grandfather lying on her bed touching her body. She began to scream uncontrollably. This time she frightened the grandfather and the young woman came into the room before he had time to escape to his room. Sarah, remembering the threat of being locked in the chicken coop, couldn't stop screaming. Thinking she was having a nervous breakdown, the foster parents took her to a hospital where she was given a sedative to calm her. A nurse with a willing ear at the hospital believed her story and she and Eugene were removed from the foster home and returned to Juvenile Court.

The children at Juvenile Court were not permitted to own anything. Each time they were returned to the Juvenile Court any small item such as a comb, handkerchief or tooth brush given to them by the foster parents would be taken away. The policy was that one child was not permitted to have possessions unless all the children had the same.

As she spoke, I cried inwardly for my brother and sister, wishing with all my heart that I could have been there to help them. I felt guilty that while I was living under our mother's care safe and unafraid, they were being subjected to such horror. Further, I felt responsible at the thought that perhaps had I not been born, they would have come home sooner. I had to tell them how sorry I was.

Mother often wrote to Sarah and Eugene keeping them informed of our situation, always with the promise of someday coming for them. They were aware of us, but we were not aware of them.

Mother had learned that John King had returned. He remarried and had taken the children to live with he, his new wife and her children. One would think this would be the end of the children's problems, however instead of finding the security and safe environment of a family life they deserved, Sarah was exposed to still more terrible experiences. So horrible that even today she cannot speak or even think of those days without becoming emotionally upset. Mother would wait no longer and starting the long proceedings to have the children put into her custody. She and Dad made many visits to the home of Mr. &

Mrs. John King before agreements were reached and Eugene and Sarah could come home.

At last I understood the reason why Sarah and Eugene carried so much sorrow, anger and mistrust inside.

CHAPTER 30

▼

In 1950, eight years after we moved, Elmer Reinhart, the boy I would eventually marry took me for a Sunday drive in his father's Plymouth. Even though it was out of the way, I asked if he would please drive down Charles Street. I had not returned nor had I seen the area since the day we moved. My heart began to beat faster and my mind was flooded with memories as we neared Hamilton Place. Elmer drove very slowly as we approached the two rows of houses.

I gasped where I saw the devastation that was then Hamilton Place. A few years before there had been a fire at #9 and the damage was too great to rebuild so it had been demolished. Tears ran down my cheeks as I gazed at the empty space where once stood the warm friendly house in which I had spent my early childhood. It appeared to have been plucked out as a dentist would remove a bad tooth. Several of the other houses were boarded up, and on the verge of being demolished. On the outside wall of a house still standing could be seen the layers of wallpaper that had decorated the fallen house. The outline of the stairs and openings in the walls that once had been a doorway. The remains of a home where a family had lived and children had played.

The wall that held back the hillside had crumbled allowing the dirt to fall onto the cobblestone street. It was as though the hillside had won the battle and was reclaiming the area from which it had been pushed back. The street light no longer dangled precariously from the pole at the far end of the rows.

We sat silently in the Plymouth, Elmer and I, gasping at the sight. I did not try to hold back the tears as I stared at what once had been my home, my growing up place. I saw the little girl I had been with long blonde hair bouncing up and down as I jumped rope. I was again roller skating on the sidewalk of Charles Street, with skate key hanging around my neck on a piece of string. Once again I walked home with my father from the streetcar stop clinging to his hand. There was mother standing in the doorway calling us to supper. My heart was breaking! A way of life had ended! I knew that I could not bring myself to come to this place again.

Only a few of the houses were still occupied. I wondered if Mrs. Clark still lived there?

From time to time I heard news of the whereabouts of some of the neighbors. One of the Fisher boys had became a butcher and in time owned his own shop in Market Place. Unknown to us at the time we moved, the Barnett family had also relocated to Geranium Street.

CHAPTER 31

▼

Today, the only proof that Hamilton Place ever existed is in the memory of the people who lived there. Five two story houses now stand on the site where once twenty-two families lived. Many of the buildings that were a special part of my life are also gone: Muellerschon's Grocery Store, Linwood School, Annunciation School, as well as the "Dinky" street car. Pleasant Valley swimming pool still remains but only through many renovations over the years.

Ironically, for fourteen years I traveled down Charles Street on the way to my job at Columbus Traditional Academy, a school which intersects Brighton Road and Charles Street. I looked straight ahead as I passed the five houses where Hamilton Place once stood. Every day I drove the same route where once I had walked with seventeen cents in my hand to buy two loaves of bread or a nickel to buy some penny candy.

Charles Street has drastically changed. Several years ago the city totally renovated the houses, and the people have returned, but the feeling is not the same.

My parents taught me to always treasure simple pleasures. If you are among those fortunate people who can still remember the thrill of jumping into a pile of autumn leaves and throwing them into the air, or the joy of throwing a snowball at an unsuspecting spouse or child, or even though you can no longer climb the steep steps you still feel the urge to go down the slide in the park, then perhaps you had your very own Hamilton Place.

I think so often of Hamilton Place and my life there. I will hold on to the memory of that special time and place knowing in my heart, that it will never come again.

0-595-26210-4